TO HAVE AND TO LOSE

MIRANDA GRANT

BY MIRANDA GRANT

WAR OF THE MYTH
Elemental Claim
Think of Me Demon
Tricked Into It
Rage for Her

FAIRYTALES OF THE MYTH
Burn Baby Burn
The Little Morgen
Bjerner and the Beast

DEATHLY BELOVED
To Have and to Lose
Death Do Us Part
For Better or For Worse

TO HAVE AND TO LOSE

This is a work of fiction. All characters are products of my imagination and should not be seen as having any more credibility than fake news does. Any resemblance to organisations, locales, or persons, living, dead, or stuck in purgatory, is entirely coincidental.

Copyright © 2022 by Miranda Grant

mirandagrant.co.uk
tiktok @mirandagrantdhromcom
Readers of the Myth (FB group)

ISBN: 978-1-914464-95-9

All rights reserved. No part of this book may be used or reproduced in any manner whatsoever without written permission by the author, except in the case of brief quotations embodied in critical articles and reviews.

Edited and published by Writing Evolution.
Interior art by Writing Evolution.

To All the People Who Can't Get Their Partner(s) Off:

Thank you for paying my bills.

TRIGGER WARNINGS ON NEXT PAGE

THIS IS A DARK HUMOUR ROMCOM AT THE HEART OF IT, SO EVERYTHING IS DONE LIGHTLY, BUT THERE ARE SOME SCENES PEOPLE MIGHT HAVE ISSUES WITH ACCORDING TO BETAS.

(THEY ARE ALSO SPOILERS, SOME MAJOR ONES)

TRIGGER WARNINGS:
Grievous Harm, Suicide, Death (including children on page), Death Jokes (including children), War

ONE

A queen does whatever it takes to win the fight.

A fair fight leads to a dead fighter.

- Aurelia

I knelt in the dark of Jace's closet, a hand over my mouth and nose, a jacket over my wasp-like wings to hide their soft glowing light. Flicking an old sock away from my position, I stifled a gag. Ugh. Did boys *not* know dirty clothes shouldn't be shoved back into the closet?

That's what under the bed was for. At least there, they could breathe.

Keeping my hand pressed over the lower half of my face, I leaned my ear against this side of the door and waited. I hated waiting, but I hated Jace more. All because his mother had died saving mine and had been a 'good friend of hers', he'd been raised in this castle with me and my siblings. Richard, my oldest brother, loved him. But me? I freaking hated him.

To Have and to Lose

For nine of my eleven years, I had been the recipient of his pranks – jerking awake to spiders crawling on me, rounding corners only to be scared shitless, being told to hold my hand out for "presents" that always turned out to be something gross. Tonight was payback.
Delicious.
Cold.
Payback.
All I had to do was wait for the scrawny jerk to get back to his room.
Then he'd open the door and get covered in yondu urine...while still dressed in his one and only army uniform. And as the newest member of Echo's strict-as-hel squadron of elite soldiers in training, he would get into so much trouble if there was even a wrinkle in his tunic. Let alone multiple bite marks and urine stains.
At the soft creak of Jace's bedroom door, my ears strained, waiting for that specific swoosh as the bucket above the mantle was tipped upside down, pulled by the string I'd wrapped around the door handle.
...
...
...
Swoosh.
"Hel's tits!"
The door banged all the way open. I grinned so hard my cheeks hurt.
Grabbing the small wire cage by my feet, I bolted out of the closet. He rubbed his blond hair with one hand and wiped at his eyes with the other. Laughing maniacally, I opened the cage and released the yondu in heat.
The small furry animal rushed him, its claws clicking across the wooden floor, its orange and black fur a fast line of evil. Opening his eyes, a ridiculously pretty teal,

Jace cursed and tried to peddle backwards, but the yondu was already humping his foot, its massive dick bumping against his boots. As he tried to swipe at it, it scurried up his trousers leg, making its way up to his balls.

"*Princess!*" he shouted as I doubled over in laughter.

Shoving both hands inside his trousers, he pulled out the yondu. It tried to fuck the air, its red dick almost as long as its body. Its little arms reached for him, its four-fingered hands grasping. Twisting its lower half, it wrapped its furry tail around Jace's wrist and started humping his arm. Looking at me, Jace smirked.

I took a step back.

"*Princess.*"

My eyes narrowed. "Why are you smi—"

Shrieking, I jumped away as he lunged towards me. If he grabbed me, I was done for. Roughly two years older than me, he was also bigger. Although I was a much better fighter (though really, anyone could beat him; he was shit), all he had to do was touch me, and the urine smell would transfer. Then the yondu would go for me too.

Sucking in a deep breath, I shouted, "Don't let him grab me!"

He cursed as Brooke, one of my two royal guards, rolled out from under his bed, her green hair flinging around her pale face. Stevie stood up from behind the sofa, a small smile pulling her lips. Together, the two young adults raced to protect me from the biggest jerk in the whole Seven Planes.

"Hey! That's not fair!" he shouted as Stevie grabbed one of his arms and Brooke the other. He looked so small between them, not even coming up to their shoulders. The yondu twisted free and ran right back to his trousers.

Skirting past him, I stuck out my tongue. "A fair fight makes a dead fighter," I said, repeating the words Brooke

To Have and to Lose

had been drilling into me from the moment I'd been born. As a potential first in line to the Raza throne (the crown going to the most capable daughter, not merely the eldest), I had been trained to fight and strategise all my life. Fairy queens did not cower; we led our armies from the front lines – just like my older sister Seqora and my mother Queen Helena were currently doing against the Vylian army up north. For two millennia we'd been fighting them – them claiming their line was the rightful heirs to our throne, us obviously not. They original rebel group had gone and made their own kingdom thousands of years ago, and still they wanted ours too.

"I'm going to get you back for this!" Jace vowed as I flew down the winding hall. Our castle was carved inside a living tree, and a lot of the rooms had been designed around the natural grain.

Laughing, I shouted, "You can try!"

But there was no way Jace was going to have any time to get me back. Even if he caught the yondu before it could chew his clothes, the piss was quickly staining. Echo would surely punish him.

And punish him she did.

For the rest of this month, Jace was stuck on latrine duty for ruining his uniform.

And gods if I wasn't going to try to convince her to make that permanent...

TWO

Defeat is for the weak.

Game. On.

— Aurelia

"*Six months*," a large man growled as he knelt over my chest, pinning me to my bed, his calloused, dirty hand over my mouth. Yanked from sleep, I came up swinging.

He blocked my first punch, but my second nailed him right in the cheek.

Cursing, he released my mouth to grab my arms. But just as I was about to scream for my guards, he pressed his hand back over my lips. "If you get Stevie and Brooke to intervene this time, I swear I'm shaving all your hair off, *princess*. Including your eyebrows."

My eyes widened. Not because of the threat – that was lame – but because of his voice. It was so much deeper than usual, I barely recognised it.

"Jace?" I mumbled against his palm.

To Have and to Lose

He scoffed. "Have you forgotten me already?"

"What happened to your voice?" Seeing how big he was now, I added, "And the rest of you?"

Even in the darkness of my room, I could make out the puff of his chest. "I hit puberty."

"Oh."

Suddenly feeling the need to squirm, I curled my toes and tensed my legs to keep myself still. When I eventually made my move and bucked him off me, I wanted it to come as a surprise. He might be a *lot* heavier than when I last saw him, but I was certain I could still best him. After all, he'd always been *so* slow. I could run laps around him if I was missing one leg, blindfolded, and half asleep.

"So as I was saying," Jace said again, his deep voice still sounding so wrong. I was used to a high-pitched squeal that kind of matched my own. "You got me six *months* of latrine duty for that dumb little prank."

"If it was dumb, you're dumber for falling for it, so ooooh, you just called yourself dumber than me. Not that I'm dumb. You're dumb."

He smirked. His hand relaxed over my mouth. "I would ask you to repeat that, princess, but all you ever talk is nonsense."

My eyes narrowed.

"So tonight, I'm getting you back for every night I had to clean the toilets. That's 203 punishments."

I rolled my eyes. "Is it going to be 203 minutes of listening to you talk? Because if so, I'd give up my crown to get out of it. Better yet, just cut off my ears."

He frowned, and I could see him warring with the decision to remove his hand so he could actually hear (and then respond to) my insults. I grinned against his palm and waited.

Lifting his chin to better sneer down at me, he dug a

hand inside his brown tunic. My eyes narrowed, then widened when he revealed a thin golden chain. It might look like the slightest tug would break it, but that was a witch's snare. Once fastened, only the voice of whoever had used it would be able to remove it.

In a sudden burst of motion, I curled my legs up. My feet wrapped around his neck. Before I could pull him backwards, he turned his head and ducked out from under my legs. He wrapped the chain around one of my ankles.

Rolling off the bed, he dragged me to the floor with him. I punched him in the face. Then elbowed. He didn't even try to block the blows, just focused on yanking me to my chair. The door to my room opened. Knowing Jace was seconds away from being torn off me by my guards, I shouted, "I've got this! Leave us."

The door closed again.

I kicked Jace in the face.

He grunted but just kept dragging me. Eventually, he managed to get me to my desk chair, where he wrapped the other end of the chain around one of the front legs. As I cursed, he pulled another golden snare out of his tunic. Hoisting me into the seat, he wrestled my arm to the armrest. Then went my other arm and leg. Heaving, I scowled at him.

When had this fucker gained so much muscle?

Standing back, he crossed his arms, a smug look on his bloodied face. "Now, *princess*, I need you to pick a body part."

I snorted. "No."

"You will. Or I'll pick for you."

My eyes narrowed. "What are you going to do? Hit me there 203 times?"

"I would never hurt you, princess." He paused. "Your mum would fucking kill me."

To Have and to Lose

Fighting back a smile, I glanced away. That she would. She wasn't known as the Harpy of Raza for nothing. But after killing Jace, she'd then kill me for being a disappointment, letting myself get tied to a chair and 'punished'.

"Pick, princess."

I rolled my eyes. "Fine, an inside thigh." There was very little chance she'd ever see that. Even if I was butt naked, hopefully the angle and shadows would hide whatever he was planning to do.

His grin was enough to worry me – not that I would ever admit it.

"So you going to actually do something," I asked dryly, "or are you just going to stand there for 203 seconds?"

His grin widened as he reached inside his tunic and pulled out a tattoo wand.

My eyes narrowed. *Fuck.*

"Spread your legs, princess, and try not to move. I'm a pretty shit artist as it is."

I wanted so badly to cross my legs. "What are you going to tattoo on me?"

He shrugged. "Whatever I can draw in 203 minutes."

Dropping to his knees, he raised the wand.

"Oh my gods," I swore as I looked down at his self-proclaimed 'masterpiece'. He'd drawn an ass on me taking a shit. And a cock pissing all over the place. In bright neon fucking colours. "Did you have to make it so big?"

He pocketed the wand, a smug look on his stupid face. "There were a lot of shits I had to clean up."

"Why?"

"Because you –"

"No, why were there a lot of shits?" I asked, looking up. "What kind of elite soldiers don't know how to use a toilet? I mean, I know you're in training, but I didn't think it was that sort of training."

He growled. "We can barely stand after a day with Echo. If we can walk far enough to the latrines, that's actually an accomplishment."

I shook my head. "And yet, you have the energy to break into my room. Maybe I should talk to her about your training."

"Don't you dare, princess."

I laughed long and hard before quieting and looking him in the eye. My gaze dropped to the godsawful masterpiece on my thigh, then rose back up. I smiled. "Oh, I so dare. Enjoy this shit-free night, Jace, because come tomorrow you'll be one of those too tired to stand up to piss."

I kept good on my promise. Perhaps a bit too good, I admitted as I watched him not move from his position on the training branch for over an hour. After that I got bored.

Flying back into the castle, inside the trunk of the tree, I left him there with all the other recruits. A smile stretched across my face.

I had so clearly won this war.

THREE

A defeated queen is a worthless queen.
I will crush you.
— Aurelia

I had, in fact, not won the war.

Over the next two years, our pranks got more and more intense.

He tore out the last two chapters of all my books.

I waxed off all the hairs on his body. *All* the hairs. Ah, I would cherish his screams forever.

He taught *all* the ravens in our aviary to fly above me and shit. We had a lot of ravens, and even though I was tall for a fairy my age, standing at a good twelve centimetres, I was still a heck of a lot smaller than a raven. One of their poops was enough to cover me from head to toe. Forty shits at once was enough to drown me.

And so I did something absolutely diabolical.

I ordered cakes to be brought to the soldiers every

night after training. Jace absolutely *loved* cake.

I then always found a way for him never to get any. It took him two months before he caught on that I was bribing the other soldiers to hold him up, to help themselves to seconds before he could get any, to 'accidentally' knock over the table holding the cakes right as he entered the canteen. Bonuses were paid to those who then stepped on them.

Once Jace finally caught on, I offered him a whole cake to himself.

The bastard was so paranoid I'd done something to it he couldn't bring himself to eat it.

So I ate it in front of him with a smile.

"Mmm, delicious."

"What do you mean there won't be any cake?" Nicholas, my youngest brother, asked as he followed me through the castle's kitchen. The idiot loved sweets so much he'd eat known poison as long as it was covered in honeydew. "You can't have an engagement party without cake," he insisted.

You could if it meant your biggest nemesis wouldn't get any. I would walk barefoot through the icy lands of Niflhel itself if it meant Jace would suffer too. Besides, it wasn't like I was that psyched about the party. I had been betrothed to Tory Deirdre of Riverall six months before I was born. I'd never even met the fairy. The only reason I was meeting her now was because I'd turned thirteen and was legally an adult, making me old enough to either agree to or refuse this engagement. After today, I probably wouldn't even see her again before the wedding.

Heading for the tray of freshly baked bread rolls, I said,

To Have and to Lose

"There will be peppered bat wings to make up for it." The baker, a man with orange hair and thin lips, gave us an evil look as he stood by the microwave, waiting for it to beep, but I ignored him and swiped two cheese rolls anyway. I tossed one to Nicholas, and he caught it with one large hand.

How was it that my brother was already bigger than me? I'd been taller than him all my life, and now, with him at only fourteen years of age, he was winning. Ugh.

"Bat wings aren't as good as cake," he complained.

No, they weren't, but Jace absolutely hated them. I wasn't the biggest fan myself, but they were growing on me.

"I'll tell you what. I'll have them bake you your own special cake if you tell me what Jace is planning."

With Nicholas having recently received his invitation (summons, really) to join Echo's squadron, I now had an inside man. Although Richard, my oldest brother at fifteen and a half, had been a member of the elite group for years now, I'd never been able to ask him to spy on Jace for me because the two were best friends – much to my absolute annoyance. And now Richard was up north fighting the Vylians, having left five months ago. Jace would've left for war at age fifteen, too, but he'd decided to stay here to train as a royal guard just so he could continue tormenting me.

"He's not planning anything." Nicholas bit into his roll and smiled.

I did the same minus the grin. I was too busy strategising. "Of course he is. He hasn't targeted me in nearly a week."

He swallowed. "That's because he's been distracted by Josie." Another bite.

"Who?"

"You know. Caroline's daughter. Has the voice of an angel. Now has the breasts to match."

I shook my head. "No way. He's never failed to torment me." Snagging another roll, I headed for the door. I didn't want to be banned from the kitchens like Jace was. "And her boobs aren't that great. They're going to give her back problems."

"More like they're going to give Jace breathing problems."

When I frowned in confusion, he held both hands up in front of him and squeezed. Then he mimed pressing them together and rubbing his face between them, his dark-blue hair flicking everywhere. I rolled my eyes. When he started pretending he was suffocating, his violet eyes bugging out of his head, I laughed.

And then my *ex-favourite* brother reached over and snagged my roll. Cramming the whole thing into his mouth, he grinned. "You seem distracted by her boobs too."

Scoffing, I shoved him away.

"That's not it," I said in absolute certainty. "That bastard's planning something big. I just know it."

Jace was planning something big all right. It just wasn't for me. It was for Josie, presumably.

Standing in the middle of his room, having snuck in through the window and having already ditched my guards (two things I was getting extremely good at these days), I looked around with a scowl. The single-sized bed was covered in dark-purple petals, the national colour of Raza, and various mushrooms were set up in vases around the place. Given their horrible arrangements, I could only presume he'd picked them himself.

I wrinkled my nose as I stared at a couple of bright purple mushrooms crammed into a yellow vase. As if *this* was what his mind had been on. It was positively insulting. Was I not a thorn in his side? Was I not a worthy adversary? Gods, if I was this unappreciated, why did I even bother? It took a lot of thought to come up with new ways to torture him. Yet, at the first possibility of boobs, he laid down his arms? Without so much as holding a summit with me to discuss a ceasefire? *The nerve.*

Oh, I was going to get him back for this. I was going to —

The door handle twisted.

"Shit!"

I headed for his closet before remembering how horrible the smell had been the last time. Turning sharply, I dived towards his bed and rolled under it just as his door opened.

Oh Hel's tits. Right in front of my face was a pile of dirty, crusty socks. Trying not to gag, I put a hand over my mouth.

"Oh, Jace, it's beautiful!"

Fuck. What the hel is she doing here? All twelve Court members and their seconds were supposed to be downstairs, enjoying the engagement party before I made my entrance. Well, "enjoying" would be a stretch. Made up of twelve women, all war heroes and ancestors of the Twelve Dragons of Kholar, the Court was a bunch of power-grabbing asshats who hated anything royal. Their seconds, usually one of their daughters, weren't much better. Then again, the Court's sole purpose *was* to stop the royal family from going mad with too much power, so it was kind of understandable, but still.

Josie was supposed to be downstairs with her mother Caroline DeGure, no doubt discussing how to get away with regicide. Not up here with Jace.

My eyes widened when I realised just where *here* was. Where *I* was. *Oh please, gods, no.* Let there be some mercy in this wretched world. Closing my eyes, I started to pray.

Aphrodite, Graeca Goddess of Love, Beauty, and Sex, please make Jace not be able to get a boner.

At the sound of wet, sloppy kisses, I prayed harder.

I will give you my first born if you give him crabs.

The bed creaked above me.

I heard Josie say she was prettier than you. Okay, that was a bit low, but I was getting desperate.

"Oh, Jace!"

Oh gods.

Grabbing two dirty socks, I balled them against my ears.

But it didn't help me when the bed started rocking above me.

Freya, Aesir Goddess of Love and War, when I'm queen, I promise I'll make your statue bigger than Aphrodite's.

"Don't stop. Gods, Jace!"

Loki! I prayed desperately.

Once known as Rumpelstiltskin, he had given an infertile couple triplets on the basis that he would get to keep one. He'd also once changed into a horse and given birth to an eight-legged foal. Although not a goddess of sex, hopefully Loki was better at answering prayers. *God of Mischief, plea–*

The creaks stopped.

As did the moans.

Slowly, I lowered the socks in my hands.

To Have and to Lose

Silence.

Thank the gods.

Well, thank Loki. Aphrodite and Freya could go screw themselves.

"You better go," Jace said as he moved off the bed, his bare feet right in front of my face.

"What? But I thought –"

"If your mum discovers you missing, she'll skin me alive. Tonight's too important for the whole Court not to be in attendance."

Her feet joined his. "Will I see you after?"

"Echo has me on guard duty."

When he leaned down to pick up her underwear, my eyes widened. My heart hammered.

But he didn't see me. Only his arm came into view.

Snatching up her dress, a dark-green piece that matched her eyes (though really, no one looked at her eyes anymore), he straightened. "Get dressed, and if you're good tonight, I'll see you tomorrow."

I fake gagged and rolled my eyes.

As their feet disappeared from view, hopefully for the door, I breathed out slowly. I needed to get out of here before Jace –

His face appeared in front of me. "Hello, princess."

Jerking up, I smashed my head against the bed frame. "*Fuck.*"

Scrambling out from under it, I jumped to my feet, rubbing the back of my head. Jace stood half-naked, his arms crossed, staring at me with a smirk.

My eyes dipped to his bare chest. Slightly damp, it gleamed in the soft light of his room – and dear gods, when had he got so fit?

"Eyes up here, princess."

Tearing my gaze up, I ignored the flaming heat of my

cheeks and lifted my chin. "I was just wondering what god you had to sacrifice your balls to to look like that."

He grinned. "You think my body's worthy of a sacrifice?"

Ugh, no. That was supposed to come out as he didn't have any balls. I clenched my teeth. "Well, you're pretty dumb, so you might as well complete your brainless hunk look."

"You think I look like a hunk." He ran his hands down his body.

I rolled my eyes. I knew I should head to the window and make it to my rooms in time to change for my engagement party, but I couldn't leave him thinking he'd won.

Because he hadn't.

At all.

Glancing down his body again, allowing myself to linger on his six-pack and the scar across his stomach, I snorted. "Poor Josie. She thought she was getting Adonis, but she just got a dud."

He crossed his arms, and I looked back up to see his smile slip into a scowl. "Dud?"

"Yeah." I shook my head with pity.

"Did you not hear her screams? Given your front row seat, princess, I would've thought –"

"Oh yeah, but come on." I snorted. "You had to know she was faking it."

His jaw ticked.

"I mean, I would too if I was a Court's second and wanted to find an easy way to spy on the royal family. And with you being Richard's best friend..." I trailed off with a cocky smile.

"She wasn't faking it."

I laughed. "You lasted like thirty seconds. You really

think you got her off in that short a time?"

He glanced away.

My smile widened.

Stepping towards him, I patted him on the shoulder as I headed for the window. "I'd say sorry, but really, you just made my night. Poor Jace can't even make a girl orgasm."

Placing my hands on the windowsill, I just started to climb out when he grabbed my arm and turned me back around.

"And how would you know what a woman sounds like when she comes?" he murmured, his grip strong on my wrist.

Trying to ignore the tingling flare of sensation crawling up my arm, I lifted my chin. "Because unlike you, *I* know how to please one." Complete and utter bullshit, but there was no way he'd know. Between pranking Jace, my fighting lessons with Brooke, and my duties as princess, which included sitting through frustrating meetings with the Court, whose ideology was kill first and don't bother asking questions *ever*, I didn't have any time for a relationship.

This whole engagement thing was only ideal because the Deirdre family had the strongest line of necromancers, and we could really use their free support up north fighting the Vylians. Their current rates were eating through our finances like a moth infestation.

"Oh yeah?" he asked.

"Yeah."

We stared into each other's eyes for long seconds, his teal set glaring, my lilac ones light with laughter. Then his gaze changed. Softened and heated all at once. His eyes dipped to my lips. My breath caught. My heart pounded faster and faster, louder and louder. His fingers around my wrist felt even tighter even though his grip had loosened.

He leaned in, and I –
　Yanked my arm free with a scowl.
　Ugh. No.
　Jace was the *last* fairy I wanted to think about like this at all.
　Turning for the window, I jumped out and spread my wings. I was *not* flying away.
　I was just...getting ready for my engagement party.

FOUR

A promised engagement is not solidified until all parties give their consent.

Consent... What consent does a princess truly have?

— Aurelia

Rubbing my hands down the thighs of my regal jumpsuit, a dark-purple piece with three gem-studded black belts criss-crossing my stomach, I took a deep breath. I didn't have time for nerves. I had a duty to my kingdom to accept this engagement.

And yet, the ornate black chain choker around my neck felt all too stiff. Nestled between my collar bones, the medallion of the Raza symbol, a raven in flight holding a snake in its talons, felt way too heavy. Like a weight dragging me all the way down to Hel.

I didn't want to marry Tory.

Simply expressing that would call off this engagement. A fairy wedding was not legalised unless all parties agreed to the marriage. If I merely hesitated before accepting, our deal would be over. It would be so easy for me to back out of the arrangement my mum had made shortly after my conception. And yet...

Drawing in a deep breath, I slowly let it out again.

I was a princess and my desires did not matter.

Otherwise, we would not be at war with three of our four neighbouring kingdoms.

We would not claim children were adults at thirteen.

We would not think art was a useless degree.

We would negotiate.

We would actually strive for peace.

Peace... My people didn't even know what that meant.

Exhaling slowly, I lifted my chin and waited for the ballroom doors to open.

"Her Royal Highness," the announcer boomed as the large hand-carved wooden doors parted in front of me. "Aurelia Emberton Foirsear Morningstar, second daughter of our treasured Queen Helena, the Harpy of Raza."

The room was completely silent as I stepped onto the top of the grand stairway overlooking the ballroom floor. The twelve Court members were dotted throughout the crowd, no doubt discussing how to put me on the throne before Seqora killed our mother. I was the "weaker" daughter in their eyes, the one they could control, the one too soft to kill my mother and sister in order to claim the crown myself. In an attempt to stop infighting while our country was at war (aka: so there wouldn't be another Vylian-like fiasco), the third queen of Raza had made it law that in order to take the throne, all other women in their immediate family had to be dead first.

The country could not be divided if there was no one else to claim the crown.

Catching my attention, a girl roughly my age moved through the crowd. Her skin was the exact shade of the tree we lived in, flawless except for lines of green ink traversing her left forearm – the proud marks of a novice necromancer. Eventually, her entire body would be covered in the tattoos of her craft.

Stopping at the bottom of the stairs, she held my gaze, and I wasn't surprised to see her eyes were a different colour – one orange, one green. A necromancer did not receive their first tattoos until after they'd called a soul back from the dead. And when that happened, one of their eyes changed forever, allowing them to see the plane of purgatory, where the dead souls resided until they made it to one of the three underworlds: Graeca, Aesir, or Gaelic.

"My promised," the girl murmured as she bowed low.

Feeling the entire ballroom on me, I inclined my head towards her. "My promised," I said back, letting her know I would be going through with the engagement ceremony later tonight. For my people. For us to hopefully end the war with the Vylians.

As the ballroom burst back into action, the live band playing something metal, Tory straightened and turned away from me. The crowd split into two, each moving to opposite sides of the mosh pit. Tory joined them, but I stayed where I was, my feet unmoving.

"You still distracted by my godly body, princess?" Jace asked, appearing beside me, armed in the black and purple uniform of the royal guard. I rolled my eyes. If being crowned meant I would have to spend all my time with him, I would beg my sister to kill me.

"Guards are to be seen, not heard," I said without turning to face him.

"That's a stupid rule. What if we need to tell you to duck?"

"Then you're not doing your job right. You should stop the threat before it ever gets that close."

He moved closer. "What if they're shooting magic?"

"Then jump in front of it without inconveniencing me."

He laughed. "That would be the most inconvenient thing for you, princess."

I snorted.

"Admit it. You'd be devastated if I was gone. You spend every free moment thinking about me."

"Thinking about how to torment you."

"Still counts."

"Where's Stevie and Brooke?" I asked, suddenly wanting them here despite having ditched them every chance I'd got these last couple of years.

"Sniper duty."

My eyes lifted to the layer of beams criss-crossing high above us. They were covered in shadows, but even if they weren't, I wouldn't be able to see them. My guards could vanish on an open plain. Sitting up there, armed with combat wands and bows, they would protect me from any threat.

"Are you waiting for me to ask you to dance, princess?"

The sudden unbidden thought of dancing with him made my stomach feel weird. I crossed my arms. "No."

"Then why haven't you joined them?" He nodded at the crowd enjoying the festivities. When I didn't answer, he asked softly, "Do you want to marry her?"

My chest tightened. I needed to say yes, no hesitation. But my lips wouldn't part. My throat wouldn't voice the words.

"You can be honest with me," Jace said. His fingers brushed mine.

My heart hammered.

"You've heard me 'fail to make a girl come'. I think we're past –"

To Have and to Lose

The large double doors at the other end of the ballroom banged open. The wind howled inside. The leaves of our tree rustled ominously. Jace jumped in front of me, his sword raised. Freeing the knives from the compartments hidden in my long sleeves, I readied myself to fight alongside him.

But it wasn't an enemy army that rushed through the doors. It was a single soldier of ours sitting on an exhausted raven. "The Vylians have entered Hare!" she shouted between breaths. "Queen Helena demands every able body to help defend the north."

"You have her letter of command?" I asked over the silent crowd.

Nodding, the woman jumped off her steed, grabbed a sealed envelope from inside her bloody tunic, and held it up so all the snipers could see it wasn't a weapon. Keeping her hands raised, she flew towards me and landed in front of Jace.

He took the letter from her and handed it to me, still in a defensive stance.

Ripping my mother's seal open, I pulled out the letter and read it quickly. My stomach dropped. The Vylians had broken through our defences. Our army was stretched too thin; no one could be spared from the other squadrons fighting the beetle-like Okahi and the snake-like Alzans. The only able bodied citizens we had left were the new recruits. The young adults – the *children* in other cultures. But a childhood was a luxury none of us had been able to enjoy for centuries. Even my spats with Jace – they had only been allowed because they taught me strategy.

Clenching the paper, I looked up at all the young faces staring back at me. "Enjoy tonight for we leave at dawn."

FIVE

A good queen understands that not all lives matter the same.

Yes they do.
— Aurelia

It took us three days to fly to the northern edge of our kingdom. Nearing Hare, my bird landed on the branches of an anaewawee tree. The thick foliage combined with the encroaching twilight limited my vision, but I could still hear the hundreds of wild birds waiting in the surrounding trees. I could hear the rodents scurrying across the forest floor as they grabbed fallen fairies – Razians or Vylians, they didn't care which, wounded or dead, it didn't matter. And above it all, I could hear the screams of my people.

"Go fuck a porcupine, you asswipe! It'd be better use of your genitals than bearing children fodder."

"Oh my gods, how could you miss? I'm missing a *fucking leg*! Here, I'll sit down to make it easier for you."

"You're as bad of a shot as that guy!"

"Gods, you make me want to kill myself out of pity."

"You missed again! Who taught you how to fight? The brownies?" The brownies were our fourth neighbour, fairies who had evolved without wings, and they were all members of a happiness-sex cult that didn't know how to wield a sword unless it was of the penis variety. And even that was debatable according to Brooke, considering they weren't allowed to provide feedback in case they 'hurt each other's feelings' – a criminal offence in Brownston.

"Do you have a plan, princess?" Jace asked as he landed beside me. "Or are we just going in to die alongside the others."

"They're not dying," I snapped, fighting the harsh beating of my pulse. Turning to my squadron, I raised my voice. "This is a rescue mission. Grab who you can and retreat. We'll retake Hare once we've regrouped."

Nudging my steed forward, I flew straight at the one-legged woman still taunting the Vylians.

Sitting down, she fought for her life, but her energy was quickly waning. With every beat of my raven's wings, her arms seemed to grow heavier. The wand she was using to protect herself wasn't moving anywhere near fast enough. When her latest spell missed the advancing Vylian, he kicked her weapon from her hand, tossing it off the branch and to the forest floor far below.

He raised his sword when I was still seconds away from helping her.

My heart twisted.

My stomach dropped.

"Jace!" I shouted instinctively, but there was nothing he could do either.

With a mocking smirk, the woman flung herself off the branch, laughing all the way down.

Pushing my heels into my raven, I ordered her into a dive. We twisted through the foliage, dodging branches, arrows, and blasts of magic. My eyes trained on the woman, a 'young adult' barely older than me, I held my breath.

And then released it as we flew past her...under her...

When I caught her in my arms, I closed my eyes for just a second. Her laughter washed through me. Using my legs, I ordered my steed to fly away.

"Where are you going?" she shouted. "I still have Vylian scum to kill!"

I tightened my hold on her before she could fling herself off the bird. "You are going to die!"

"You brought a necromancer, right?" Twisting out of my arms, she dived for the floor. She spread her wings, dodged a pack of rats on the ground, and snatched her wand up from between them. Shooting a spell at her leg, she shot up the trunk of the tree.

I blinked in awe as the skin started to mend over her cauterised stump.

"Gawk later, princess!" Jace snapped as he flew beside me. Throwing a knife in front of me, he deflected an arrow that had been shot in my direction.

I tried my hardest not to look impressed. It would only go to his head. Ordering my raven to turn back around, I nocked my bow with an arrow and shot a Vylian ready to stab one of ours in the back.

"Retreat!" I shouted as I flew around the tree. "We'll regroup at Rokni!"

The Vylians didn't have the numbers to chase us, not if they didn't want another of our squadrons to come in behind them, retake Hare, and slaughter them from the back.

It took me a few passes around the tree, but eventually,

the word spread. Only the legless woman was left. Surrounded by a number of Vylians, she wouldn't live long. My sister would have left her. So would've my mother.

But I was neither of them.

Nudging my raven, I flew back to save her a second time. Shooting past me, Jace threw a flurry of knives, each one landing in a Vylian heart. As they tumbled to the forest floor, he grabbed the woman, choked her out, and flew back towards me.

Nodding my thanks, I retreated with my soldiers.

"Look who I saved," Brooke teased as she entered the pub in Rokni we were using as a command centre. I glanced up from the map marked with Razian and Vylian troops in front of me. Grinning, I spread my wings and leaped across the table to slam into the dark-haired man behind her.

"Dickie!" My arms roped around him.

Holding me tightly, my oldest brother kissed the top of my head just like he'd used to do when I was young, after singing me to sleep whenever I'd had a day of hard training. Which was always. Brooke was a beast of a teacher.

"*Kultara*," he teased. It was ancient Gaeric, meaning 'thorn in my side', and something he'd been calling me for years.

Pulling back, I slugged him in the shoulder, but my smile never fell. "Glad you're not dead yet."

"Glad your squadron's here. We can't retake Hare on our own."

"Clearly," Jace said as he came up to us. He wrapped

Richard in a hug, then lowered a hand down to his ass.

"Fuck off, Jace." Slipping free, Richard shoved him back. Under Jace's laughter, my brother turned to me. "Is Nicholas here?"

I shook my head. "Mother ordered him to stay behind to continue our line if need be." Although under normal circumstances, a male and his heirs weren't recognised as being pure enough to lead (so their numerous unknown offspring couldn't have claim to the throne). But if Nicholas was the only surviving member, the Court would allow it. They might not like us on a personal level, but they wouldn't let our line die in fear of a civil war. And if that happened, the snake-like Alzans and the beetle-like Okahi would destroy us once and for all. Although we currently had them pushed back the furthest they'd been for centuries, they would only need a crack in our defences to regain all the territory they'd lost.

"Good." When Richard's gaze shifted to the table of maps, I led him to it.

Pointing to Selz, a few trees over from Rokni, he said, "Seqora is here." He tapped Emirin; it was well into Vyla territory. "Queen Helena is here."

"Then we have to save her."

He glanced up. "Even if we manage to get to her, we do not have the numbers to make it back out."

"But we have to try. She's our mum!"

"She is queen and queens die. Seqora will see to that soon." His lips tightened. His voice lowered. "It is because of her that Queen Helena is there. If she manages to secure Emirin, it'll be a great victory, but the odds of that are slim."

He pointed to Hare. "Retaking this city will give us the best position to hold this area. If the Vylians find their way into our armoury and open it, they'll kill us all."

To Have and to Lose

I frowned. "Why? What's in it?"

His jaw worked tight. He glanced first at Jace, then at me. "Bees."

"Fuck." Bees were poisonous to us all. One sting would kill an adult fairy, and hojun bees (those native to this area) went on rampages, stabbing everything that moved, not caring that they'd die too when their stingers got stuck in their victims.

Richard exhaled strongly. "And they're warded to explode on contact."

"What?" The ever loving fuck. "Who signed that off?"

"Seqora." His violet eyes held mine, speaking things he would not say.

Our sister had finally gone mad.

And after she killed mum, she would be coming for me.

Fearing she would release the bees herself if she was the one to retake Hare, I pointed to the map. "After we retake this, we hide the beehive somewhere else."

Richard looked at me, and I knew he wanted me to give the order to destroy it, but I couldn't. The bees hadn't asked to be a part of this war.

Neither had I.

We didn't quite have the numbers to retake Hare, so at midnight, I ordered a retrieval crew to pick up any useable corpses for Tory to revive. Within a week, her tattoos had spread across her whole arm, and we had a good-sized addition to our squadron.

The one-legged woman, having crafted a wooden leg with the words 'fuck you' carved down its length, joined us a few hours before dawn the day we were to retake Hare. Looking at Jace, she nodded at his stomach. "I should've stabbed you harder."

"Your mother tells me that every day."

Frowning, I glanced between them. He had risked his life for her. *Does he like her like he does Josie?* Josie had been left behind in Kholar given her duties to the Court, but most fairies had open relationships given the distance caused by war.

I scowled as the woman stepped towards me. Her eyes light, she held out a hand. "I'm Evangeline, Petre's youngest daughter and proud deliverer of Jace's first scar."

The urge to growl at her clawed at my throat. Forcing my hand out, I shook hers. Petre was a member of the Court, and although the twelve members were all technically equal, she was their silent leader. Looking into Evangeline's silver eyes rimmed with green, I could see the resemblance. And like her snake of a mother, she'd hurt Jace.

Worse, she was *proud* of it.

As if feeling the tension rising inside me or maybe just hearing the weird growl escaping my throat, Jace stepped in between us. "Careful, princess," he murmured with a smile, "you wouldn't want to make me think you cared."

Glaring at him, I turned away. "The only thing I care about is winning this war."

Pulling myself onto my raven, I flew towards Hare with the strongest desire to kill something.

SIX

War is glorious.

> *What is glorious about dead children?*
> *— Aurelia*

Darting through the branches on top of our ravens, we made our way towards Hare under the cover of darkness. The magical light network of the city had long been ruined, and no one wanted to waste their magic to bring it back online. So now, the only lighting was via beambugs and bioluminescent moss held in glass lanterns. Soft glows that didn't reach far.

Richard and his squadron flew in front of me and mine, the more experienced soldiers at the front. Jace, Brooke, and Stevie surrounded me in a spearhead of protection. Nearing Hare, we split into multiple groups to come at the city from various directions. Evangeline led the smallest team, made up of only two other witches (all we had) and herself. Their role was to dart around the tree, causing as much chaos with their magic as they could before flying off, disorientating the Vylians about what parts needed protecting.

My blood rushing fast through my veins, I clenched my fist around my bow.

"Relax, princess," Jace said, and I shot him a scowl.

"I am," I snapped, my nerves more fried than I'd ever admit. I had been trained in combat since I was two, as all fairies were. I was ready for this. Ready to protect my people, our kingdom.

Forcing my fingers to relax, I took a deep breath and pulled an arrow from my quiver. As I commanded my steed with my knees, I nocked the arrow but didn't draw back.

In no time at all, we passed the one tree between us and Hare. A Vylian squatted on one of the outer branches, his trousers around his ankles as he leaned forward to wipe his ass. His head whipped up, meeting my eyes just as he brought forward the brown-stained tissue. He fumbled with the warning horn at his waist, but in his panic, he raised the wrong item to his lips.

I gagged at the same moment he did, somehow able to taste the toilet paper myself.

"Eat shit!" Brooke shouted beside me as she released her own arrow. It flew straight into his mouth, lodging into the back of his throat. If he didn't yank it out before he died, the poor bastard was going to be judged in the afterlife with an arrow of shit in his throat.

The soft snickers that passed Stevie's and Brooke's lips, though, soon died as a horn blared somewhere to our right. A second one sounded. A third. A fourth. And in seconds, the tree was alive with an angry horde of fairies coming to beat us back.

Drawing my bow, I shot at an advancing Vylian. A

shield of blue magic erected in front of him, catching the arrow and then quickly shattering. His magic was weak, and I nocked and let fly another projectile before he could use any more. My shoulders tensed as I watched the wooden shaft dig into his chest. He screamed as he slumped to the ground, a terrible sound that reached inside my lungs and squeezed. He was so scared, and in this moment, he wasn't a Vylian anymore. He was just a young fairy robbed of a future.

A future I was taking.

My cheeks hot, I nocked another arrow and let it fly. This one hit his heart, a quick kill. My first kill...

He slumped to the ground, the wand in his hand rolling to the edge, his life bleeding free. His eyes stayed open and on mine, terrified and alone.

My mouth filled with a bitter tang as my fingers tightened on my bow. Noise faded for just a moment. The world focused only on him.

Swallowing hard, I jerked my gaze away from him, forcing the regret down. The world exploded in sound and focus once more, the chaos of battle reigning all around me.

Jace grunted as a Vylian raven slammed into his, taking him away from me. Heart in my throat, I nocked another arrow and let it fly.

"Fucking *pr*–" he shouted as my arrow flew past his cheek. "*-ick*!" he finished, changing his scream of 'princess' at the last second so the Vylians wouldn't realise my worth.

My mouth dropping, I fumbled for another arrow. *I won't miss this time.*

And I didn't.

I nailed him right in the arm.

Well, skimmed it rather than embedded, but I was still

counting that.
 Only...
 The 'him' I'd hit had been Jace...
 "Stop helping me!" he shouted as he shoved his knife into his adversary, then shouldered him off his steed. The Vylian's raven cawed angrily as it attacked Jace's bird. I didn't want to kill it —animals were innocent— but swallowing down my morals, I nocked another arrow.
 For Jace.
 But they were moving too fast, and my hands were so damp.
 I can do this.
 Exhaling slowly, combating my stress, I released my arrow.
 Cursing, Jace jumped from his bird, barely missing getting hit in the face, and let the two ravens battle it out amongst themselves. Flying back to my side, he glared at me.
 My cheeks heating, I lifted my chin. "Don't just fly there! Kill some Vylians!"
 His eyes narrowing on me, he pulled out a knife. "This is how you fucking help someone," he growled and tossed it into the Vylian attacking Stevie.

 The battle was over.
 My hands shook, my body flooded with adrenaline, my mind unable to grasp the fact that the fighting was finally over.
 As my eyes skirted around the bloody branch, my limbs wanting nothing more than to collapse in a state of utter exhaustion, I swallowed thickly.
 My people staggered around me, bloodied and bruised

To Have and to Lose

and dying. Stevie and Brooke were going around with healing wands, having already healed me. Jace stood in front of me, his hands still holding his knives, his teal eyes looking at me funny, but my attention was constantly being diverted. My mind wild in the sudden unnatural silence.

I'd been schooled in the ways of war long before I could speak. I'd learned how to lift a blade before I was properly potty trained. I'd been taught war was glorious, honourable, a thing to look forward to and brag about when you came home (if you were so lucky).

But I'd never been taught about the screams. The half-dead bodies trying to drag themselves to cover as magic, swords, and arrows whooshed around them. The rough pounding of your heart as you tried to fight soldiers way above your experience, as you were beat onto your ass and nearly killed before your bodyguard stabbed him in the back. The panic making you shake as you realised your squadron might not survive, a squadron *you* were responsible for, because one by one, those beside you fell, their screams silenced forever.

My eyes landed on our steeds as they moved in purpose across the branches. My stomach dropped. My soul heaved.

And they had never mentioned *our* ravens hopping from corpse to corpse indiscriminatingly, eating their fill as we stood heaving, covered in blood, some ours, some theirs, our weapons still half raised despite somehow being the winners. The fear pulsing through us, the sickness in our stomachs, the guilt, the pain, the absolute horror.

"Princess..."

Dropping my sword, I looked all around me. At the blood-stained branches. At the body-littered floor. Despite having finally taken Hare back after three weeks of bloodshed, it did not feel like a victory.

Strong arms came around me.

Leaning into them, I shifted my gaze to the trunk of the great tree.

But at least they had not managed to release the bees.

No one would have survived then.

Closing my eyes, I pulled away from Jace and picked up my sword.

I was a fairy princess, and we did not have the luxury to break.

While rescuing my mother the next week, I lost a hundred and sixteen soldiers. A hundred and sixteen *children*.

Fog rolled in and we got separated.

Later, I found bits of their corpses.

Richard had told me it would be a suicide run, but I had not listened.

Screaming, I watched Brooke fall to her knees as we fought our way out of Emirin, a sword through her chest. Ducking under the magical blast of a wand, I threw a knife at the Vylian who had attacked me. Not waiting to see if it killed him, I jumped over a body and ran towards my guard. Her eyes met mine. A smile turned up the edge of her lips. And then her head was gone, cut from her body in one stroke.

Launching into the air, I flew after her head. Catching it, I threw it at the Vylian responsible. It slammed into his face, knocking him off the branch. He didn't manage to fly before hitting the ground; then the rats tore him to pieces.

To Have and to Lose

    Coming up beside me, my mother laughed. "Brooke would've loved that. She killed a man by *giving him head*. She always was such a whore."

SEVEN

A queen never surrenders.

This war will never end.

— Aurelia

Four years.

Four fucking years of going back and forth with the Vylians and nothing changed. Each fight was the same. Some we lost. Some we won. Some we won, but they felt like a loss. And now, here we were: right back where we'd been years ago – fighting to take back Hare.

The only difference was the new faces.

I didn't recognise half of them beside me anymore.

EIGHT

War is a necessary evil.

It's a pointless evil.
- Aurelia

"Are you okay?" Jace murmured behind me as I knelt beside a bucket of water inside the rubble of my new 'home'.

I nodded, scrubbing at the blood on my leather cuirass laid out on the floor. A Vylian, younger than me by a few years, had fallen against me today, his eyes wide with terror. One of my soldiers had stabbed him in the neck as we'd retaken Hare. Their knife had still been there, clutched between his shaking fingers. Fighting back the rage threatening to flow down my cheeks, I pressed my fingers harder into the rag.

"You should blot, not –"

"I've got it!" I snapped, scrubbing faster, breathing harder.

He knelt down beside me. I ignored him.

His fingers came over mine. I turned to deck him with my other fist.

He let it hit him in the face, and I stilled, shocked at the pain shooting up my fingers. Over the last four years, we'd traded light teasing punches, much tamer than our youthful spats of war, but this one was different. This one was hard and full of an agony I couldn't face. "You said you'd never hurt me."

The words tumbled out, and I wasn't even sure why I'd said them. He hadn't hurt me at all; I could barely feel the pain anymore. And yet, tremors still wracked me. My vision blurring, I looked at him in horror.

The fuck if I'm going to cry in front of him.

I jumped to my feet, but he pulled me back down. Ripping the rag out of my hand, he started dotting at the leather. "Do you want all of the blood off?" he asked, not looking at me. "Or just this stain?"

Blinking my eyes dry, grateful his were still lowered, I looked at my cuirass. Stains were everywhere – the only memories left of all those who had died around me. "Can you get it all?" I rasped.

"It'll take a few passes." He dipped the rag into the bucket of water, turning it pink.

But I heard what he didn't say. Tomorrow, it would be stained afresh.

Glancing away, I tried to tell myself that a dead Vylian was a good thing. It was them or us. Them or Richard. Them or Jace. Or Stevie. Or Evangeline. *A dead Vylian is a good thing.*

"I'm sorry I hit you," I murmured.

He finally looked up, his teal eyes soft and just the slightest bit wet. A smirk tugged at his lips. "You've been hitting me for years, princess. Truth be told, I've started to like it."

His eyes dipped down my body, leisurely and hot.

I stepped back, crossing my arms, and wished the leather cuirass was back on me – bloodied or not.

A chuckle blew through his lips, and he ducked his head as he started blotting at my armour again. "Go get some sleep, princess."

Shifting uneasily, I took a step back.

I wasn't retreating. I was just...tired.

Gods, I was so fucking tired.

A good night's sleep hadn't helped. Pulling myself out of bed of whomever's house I'd commandeered here, I reached for my trousers. My arm froze as my fingers grazed the leather. There weren't any stains on them.

Grabbing them, I flipped them over. Not a single dot marred them.

Looking towards the living room, where I'd left Jace last night, I found it empty. My cuirass was hanging up over the back of a chair near the far wall, in front of a small desk. Placing my feet on the wooden floor, I skirted around the sofa and made my way over to it.

"Morning, princess."

"Shit!" Jumping, I spun around to face the sofa. Jace was stretched out on it, one arm behind his head, his chest bare. I'd not seen him shirtless often, and my eyes snagged on his smooth abs as a flicker of heat bloomed in my belly. My gaze dipped to the scar on his stomach –the one Evangeline had given him– and narrowed even as my lips parted. There was a twitch of movement below his wa–

"Eyes up here, princess."

My gaze shot up as my cheeks heated.

"And you really need to learn to watch your back."

"That's what you're here for," I snapped, irritated I had missed him. He was never going to let me live this down. "You got all the stains out," I said, lifting up my trousers. As his eyes drifted to them, he sat up, and I was intensely aware I was dressed in only my long shirt.

My chest tight, I struggled to keep my eyes and feet where they were as a new strange energy urged me to move.

"You did say you wanted them all out."

"What else did you do to them?" I asked, pretty freaking certain he'd soaked them in yondu urine or something. Jace was never 'just nice'. In the four years we'd been here, the both of us had called a cease fire on our prank war and in the mask of night, we talked about stuff, but this was more than just a white flag. This was... *I don't know, but I don't like it.*

"Nothing. I promise."

I looked at the trousers warily, trying to figure out what he was hiding. When he stood, I tensed, ready to defend myself from whatever new prank he had planned.

"Here." He reached for the leather in my hands, and my fingers tightened on them instinctively. "I'm just going to show you they're fine."

Looking into my eyes, he shoved an arm down one of the legs. I sucked in a breath, expecting some magic or another to erupt around him, hitting me with something vile.

But there was nothing.

Just him standing in front of me, his hand in my trousers, his chest bare and gleaming with the summer heat, and his eyes holding mine.

Fuck...me.

To Have and to Lose

Now I knew how he'd felt when I'd eaten that cake in front of him. My body burned with an energy I couldn't explain, each raised hair making me hypersensitive to his movements, his plans.

Begrudgingly accepting there was nothing wrong with my trousers, though, I yanked them out of his hands and bent down to put them on. Realising I was about to hit his chest with my face, I snapped, "Do you mind?"

"Not at all."

He stood there, not moving, and I stilled to glare up at him. My pulse thrumming against my ribs, I scowled at how close he was. Before I could tell him to step the fuck back, though, the door to the outside opened. My eyes widened as I realised how this looked. Me, bending down to seemingly take off my trousers. Him, standing there shirtless, his chest close to my lips.

And shit, now that thought was in my mind...

Smirking, Jace turned, and my eyes dipped to his ass. To his tight, delicious ass.

Ugh. No. This is Jace, remember?

Annoying fucking Jace.

"Morning, Richard," he said, just his voice managing to irritate the hairs on my neck in this moment. "You bring us breakfast?"

Cursing at the unwanted thought of breakfast with Jace (what was wrong with me this morning?), I shoved my legs through my clothes and turned to grab my cuirass. Pushing past the most annoying person in the world, making sure to shove my shoulder into him, I looked at my brother. "Let's go."

He glanced between me and his best friend, his eyes hard, one hand going to the sword at his hip. "Command can wait. What were you and Jace –"

"Fuck off, Dickie." Shoving past him, too, I made my

way outside.

For once, Jace didn't follow me immediately, but I was certain he was watching me from one of the windows of my 'home'. Holding my arm up behind me, I held up two fingers, flicking him off.

I could almost hear his laughter as I walked across the branch and entered our new command hub.

The two idiots joined us a few minutes later. As I talked to Tory, going over our numbers, I could feel Jace's eyes on me. He was always watching me, but this time it felt different. Shifting, I fought the urge to look over at him. The last thing I needed was to see him smirking over my 'retreat'.

Stevie sat at the table with us, maps spread out in front of her. As the oldest, most experienced person in our squadron, her responsibilities had shifted from royal guard to lieutenant and advisor this last year. Evangeline leaned back in her chair beside her, her feet kicked up on the table, her ankles crossed, her prosthetic limb on top. She tossed a gosberry at Jace while she ate her own. He had a ridiculous love for them.

I frowned, wondering if she 'gave him' anything else he loved. My eyes slipped from Tory to her.

Grinning, Evangeline winked at me.

Scowling, I looked back at the necromancer. Her report was done, though, and now she was staring at my brother. No longer betrothed, she had taken up an interest in basically everything that moved. Although, saying that, I didn't know her well enough to know if she would've stopped had our engagement not been interrupted. She was selfish and she was greedy, but she was also a damn good necromancer.

Standing, I leaned over the map Stevie was studying. She glanced at me briefly before trailing her finger through the trees of northern Raza and into Vyla. "Emirin is a day's hike from here. It'll be best to go on foot and fly low over the river. They won't be expecting us to pass that way."

"That's because it's suicidal," Richard cut in, leaning over the table behind Stevie. "You'll have to pass a dozen of their trees. They'll have sentries."

"Which is why we need to pass them at night. If we leave here at noon, we can wait in the underbrush until we have adequate cover. The moon isn't out tonight."

"Rats and snakes are," he pushed.

"And yondus," Jace added. "They're in heat at the moment."

Glancing down at my chest, really, *really* hoping he hadn't done anything to my leather, I shook my head. "This is our best chance to end this war. King Dravr was spotted there yesterday morning."

Despite my words, I did not truly believe that killing the Vylian king would end this. Just how them killing Mother would not stop this pointless slaughter. But I had to try something. I was tired of losing so many people.

My eyes flicked to Jace, lingered for just a moment too long.

Standing, I looked at my brother. "I'm doing this. The command is yours in my absence."

I kept the squadron small – just Jace, Evangeline, Tory, and me. Evangeline for her magic, Tory for her necromancy, and Jace because I couldn't fucking shake him. Richard flew down with us to the roots of the tree, his face speaking all the words he wouldn't say.

That none of us would say.

For every day, we had the chance of dying, and today was no different.

Turning from him, I headed off into the underbrush. Every rustle of leaves and twigs caused my nerves to spike. My blood pounded under my skin, seemingly shaking my whole body. I could feel it beating in my toes, my ears, my teeth. Forcing my breaths to stay level, I fought the urge to fly into the air, away from all the dangers of the forest floor.

Snakes and spiders were already out, as were centipedes, ifikos, frogs, lephers, and countless other creatures willing to eat us. At twilight, there would be many more: rats, foxes, vixens... The list was extensive.

Stopping us once we neared the ever-changing Vyla-Raza border of our kingdom, Evangeline ordered us all to strip. We did so without hesitation, though my eyes kept flicking over to Jace. He had a few more scars on his body. A small incision in his chest had been given to him by Richard during one of our 'victory' celebrations. The idiot had convinced my brother he could catch a throwing knife.

He most definitely could not.

Although most fairies passed their ascensions at puberty, allowing their bodies to heal from wounds and no longer scar, Jace had hit his late. It wasn't until a couple months ago that he'd finished his ascension, his body now full of dormant magical energy that lived in all of us.

As my hands went to my leather waistband to pull down my trousers, they stilled with sudden clarity. The fucking tattoo Jace had given me was there in bright neon fucking colours. I'd picked the inner thigh, hoping it couldn't be seen, but he'd drawn it fucking massive.

My teeth clenching, I glared at him while he smirked at me.

"Something wrong, princess?" His pretty teal eyes twinkled, and I wished so hard to carve them out.

"Not at all," I said, yanking my trousers down. I kept his gaze, daring him to say something, but when his attention lowered, I suddenly wanted him to say everything.

What the hel?

My body flushing with a heat so intense it irritated my skin, I ducked my head and quickly stepped out of my clothes. I tried to ignore the prickles inside, but my lungs tightened with their blatancy. Jace was no longer my enemy, more like a friend, but he was still *Jace*.

Annoying fucking Jace.

And I'd be damned if he made me feel anything other than some level of irritation.

Even if he had spent all night cleaning out stains that would quickly return. A pointless endeavour he'd done for me...

I shifted, my limbs restless, my body feeling as if it was poised on the edge of...*something*. Pulled to him, I looked up.

Jace's eyes were still on me, unmoving and yet moving too much in their intensifying heat. The blood-free leather of my attire became more prominent under his gaze.

More meaningful than just an order I had given my guard.

Swallowing, I ducked my head, breathing fast and shallow.

Evangeline laughed for a split second before biting it back so she didn't give away our position. Refusing to look at her or Tory or *Jace* again, I snapped, "Just get on

with it. Time is precious."
My skin itched, and I hated it.
And yet...wanted more?
He'd cleaned off all the blood...
Lost a night of sleep...
And gods, the way he was looking at me now –
"Very *precious*," Jace murmured, catching my breath in the palm of his fist. And like a fool, I looked up at him.
Shit...
The heat I'd been trying to keep down moved into my mouth. My lips parting, I flicked my tongue out to combat the sudden dryness shooting down my throat, but all that did was give the heat a way out. It jumped to Jace, filling his eyes, connecting us with a bridge of its flames.
Flames I couldn't smother.
And then his eyes dipped low, aiming the heat everywhere he looked. My cheeks burned, my lips, my throat, the top curves of my breasts beneath my bra. I struggled not to pant, to remind myself that this was *Jace* of all people.
But then the heat was burning through the *blood-free* thin material covering my breasts, brushing my nipples with an intensity that left them hard. And *gods*, I wanted to take a step forward at the same time as wanting to step back. There was a danger to playing with fire.
And Jace was a fucking inferno.
Tory's sudden yelp of pain shattered the bridge connecting me to Jace. Turning to her, my body flush and sucking in air, I watched as she dropped onto all fours, her body shifting into that of an ifiko lizard. Black scales erupted across her body as a long tail started growing out of her ass. Her arms and legs spread out, cracking as the bones popped during their shift. Opening her jaw, she flashed small sharp teeth as she hissed and flicked her

To Have and to Lose

new forked tongue.

With a wave of her wand, Evangeline caused Tory to glow a soft green. "We'll have three hours before the spell wears off," she said as she turned to me. "That should get us to the river."

Unhooking my bra and undoing the ties at the sides of my underwear, I kept my eyes off Jace. But I could still feel his on me, feel the importance of the stain-free clothes at my feet.

With a deep breath, I blocked him out and prepared myself for the pain.

My bones snapped under my skin as I dropped to the ground. Squeezing my eyes shut, I struggled not to scream. Shifters went through this pain all the time, I told myself. I could suffer it twice in my life – once now and once when we shifted back into our fairy forms.

Opening my new mouth, I panted through it, my body heaving on hard shudders. I flexed my toes and flicked out my tongue as I looked over my new self. Everything but my mind and senses were different. Those stayed the same as a true transformation was a power reserved only for the gods.

Evangeline changed Jace, then collected our clothes and weaponry into a bag. After strapping it to Tory, she shifted herself, and the four of us scrambled towards the river.

One way or another, this war was going to end.

And then perhaps, maybe... My eyes flicked to Jace.

Maybe I wouldn't have to watch anyone else die.

Slipping across the forest floor, we snuck into the Vylian kingdom. The trees were the same, but the air felt different. Polluted and icy, it burned my lungs. My scales itched with a need to leave this place, to turn back before we were spotted and executed.

If we were so mercifully dealt with.

If they discovered our identities, I would be tortured for years just as their morale boost, and Tory would be forced to work for them. Necromancers were rare, and one from her line was worth more than a squadron of their own soldiers. Evangeline had pissed them off so much these last few years, they actually had a ridiculously high bounty on her head. She didn't just kill the enemy; she made a laughing stock out of them first.

On one of our retreats from Hare, she had started fighting a Vylian commander. She'd used her magic to root him in place, and then instead of giving him an honourable death in battle, she had yanked down his underwear and shrunk his penis...while giving him the massive balls of a rat. With his trousers stuck around his ankles, he hadn't been able to pull them up, and his screams of rage had comforted us through the night in the next tree over.

When we had retaken Hare in a couple more weeks, his black trousers had still been there, as well as a message to Evangeline: *The next time I see you, I will kill you.*

He'd seen her again in the next battle...where he'd fallen for the exact same trick. His tiny penis shrunk even further as his balls expanded to the size of his fists.

Laughing, she'd left him there until the next time we lost Hare and his people could come back to free him.

But at least Jace...Jace was a no one to them. He would die quickly.

Nearly three hours later, we made it to the river. Tory shifted first, wearing just the backpack. She swung it off,

To Have and to Lose

dug though to grab each of our underwear, and tossed them at us. The transition hurt just as much going back into my fairy form, and I nearly cried out when my wings popped out of my back.

Crouched over on my hands and knees, I shuddered as I breathed through the pain. I donned my underwear and bra before standing, wincing as every movement sent sharp pains down my spine.

"So who's your tattoo artist?" Evangeline asked. She and Tory grinned, staring at my thigh.

Ignoring them, I fluttered my wings and shook out my arms and legs. Cracking my neck, I twisted my torso and took a step towards the bag.

Evangeline snatched it up first and held it away from me, her eyes sparkling. "Did Jace do it?"

"We're on a mission, Ev. We don't have time for this."

"We're probably going to die soon. This is the only time we'll have –"

I lunged for the bag. Chuckling, she released it to me.

"You need to work on your penmanship, Jace, before I ever let you anywhere near my body."

I gritted my teeth as I shoved a hand into the bag.

"That was a couple years ago. I'm sure I've improved."

I snorted. The only thing he'd improved at was pissing me off. Grabbing my trousers, I shoved my legs through, then reached for my shirt.

"Oh yeah? Maybe when we get back then, you can give me a tattoo...here."

I absolutely refused to see where she was pointing. I didn't care what Jace did with his wand. He could touch the whole freaking squadron with it, and I wouldn't care. At all.

"What will I get out of it?" Jace asked, causing my throat to fill with a growl. The last three hours of running in silence, with nothing but my thoughts to torment me, hadn't helped curb the new fire growing inside me.

It didn't make sense for things to have changed between us just because he'd cleaned up some blood...did it?

"Well," Evangeline said slowly, her voice deepening into a purr. "I'm sure we can come to an agreement."

Snapping my head up, I glared at her as I finished donning my cuirass. "Jace won't have the time. He has a lot of duties to attend to."

She grinned at me, not the slightest sign of disappointment in her eyes. Laughing, Tory shook her head as she reached for the bag. I tossed it at her, much harder than I'd meant to, and for some dumb reason that set her off even harder.

I hissed at her to be quiet.

Biting her cheeks, she obeyed immediately, but her eyes still shone as bright at Evangeline's.

Ugh.

Turning, I looked towards the river, but my gaze was snagged by Jace. Standing in just his briefs, his eyes tracked me, always watching. A slow smile curled his lips as he, too, looked at where the tattoo was. And despite now being fully clothed, I felt more naked than I ever had before.

Something *had* changed between us. I could feel it in every part of me.

His eyes back on mine, he took a step forward.

A slow beat grew rapidly stronger, pulsing between my ears, seemingly moving my whole body. My lips parted as the heat from earlier erupted in my belly. My toes curled, digging into my boots, keeping me standing as the slightest of shivers shot down my legs.

With every step he took, it got harder to breathe until

To Have and to Lose

my lungs stuttered to a complete stop.

I wanted...

I want...

I had no idea what exactly, but when he dipped his head, his eyes on my lips, that felt like a damn good start. A slow exploration into new territory. Just a moment of curiosity...

I lifted my chin just the slightest bit.

A slow smile spread across his cheeks.

He raised a hand to my face, his eyes hot and unwavering.

The pulse in my ears drowned out even the roar of the river as my eyes started to flutter...

Blooping my nose, he passed me, his grin breaking free completely.

I blinked a few times as my mouth fell open.

Spinning, I balled my fists and watched as he grabbed the bag off Evangeline. Pulling clothes out of it, he got dressed quickly, then pivoted to face me.

That fucking smirk of his was still there.

Glaring at him, I faced the river.

His soft chuckle sent goosebumps down my spine.

Shaking them off me, I spread my wings and launched into the air. My eyes tracked the water as I flew over it, searching for any shadows moving beneath. A fish could easily swallow me whole, though right at this moment, that did not seem like too much of a bad thing.

As if I'd almost let Jace kiss me.

As if I'd let him *know* he could've kissed me.

Ugh. He was so...

So...

Ugh!

I banked hard, just registering the shadow before it jumped out to grab me. Water sprayed across my wings, the force sending me careening with wild flaps. Struggling to stay in the air, I pumped hard, my chest heaving from the effort. Jace shot below me, ready to catch me, and I thought about diving deliberately just to piss him off.

But this mission was too important to risk.

Straightening as the fish landed back in the water, I looked at my guard and nodded once. I was fine despite the harsh beating of my heart – though if I was honest, I don't think that had been caused by the fish...

Shaking such stupid thoughts free, I concentrated on the river. I didn't need any more close calls.

By the time we landed, my body buzzed everywhere, the adrenaline from that flight seeping out of my pores. Every three freaking seconds, it seemed, a fish had jumped up trying to grab one of us. Thank gods, none had come close.

Looking up at the trees around us, I listened to the cries of war. They were soft and distant but just as fierce as always.

"We wait here until nightfall," I said. Well into Vylian territory, every tree would have sentries. But with luck, they'd only be watching the skies. Unlike us, they didn't fight the snake-like Alzans or the beetle-like Okahi who ran across the forest floor like an infestation.

"Those rocks look like a good bet," Evangeline said as she headed for a small pile of them. She pulled out her wand and flicked it in the air. After a second, she nodded. "It's clear."

Lowering my wings, keeping them tight against my back, I scrambled through one of the gaps. It wasn't roomy inside by any means, but it would do.

Lying down, I rested my head on my arms and closed my eyes. Sleep was a precious thing that came quickly.

NINE

Weaknesses should be eliminated before they can be used against you.
Jace is not a weakness...
— *Aurelia*

I woke to complete darkness a few hours later, a hand on my leg. Jace always woke me by shaking my thigh, a silent code so I would know if I needed to come up swinging.

Rolling onto my side, I sat up and stretched out my arms as I cracked my neck. Jace's hand still on my leg, I turned to look at his silhouette. Nodding at me, he removed his hand, and I jumped to my feet, needing to move. "Is everyone ready?" I asked, waiting for my eyes to adjust.

When everyone confirmed, we snuck out of camp and headed for Emirin, for the Vylian king who would not see the morning sun.

Saving her magic, Evangeline didn't transform us

again. We needed her at full strength to sneak us into Emirin, and I didn't like the idea of being caught mid-shift with my pants down – or immediately after, when I was struggling to move through the pain. If we got cornered, I wanted us able to kill ourselves quickly.

The forest was eerily quiet as we moved through it. My stomach in knots, I looked at Jace beside me. A slight frown pulled him down as he swivelled his head, his eyes narrowed.

My heartbeat sped up.

My palms dampened.

Touching the hilt of one of my knives, I walked a bit faster.

Jace fell behind me just by a few steps, taking up the rear in case whatever was hunting around here found us. It had to be big and lethal given how quiet everything was. All I could hear was us.

A sudden feral scream pierced the air behind me. Jumping, I twisted around and pulled out my knife, my heart in my throat, my blade raised.

"Relax, princess," Jace grinned. "It's just a yondu's mating call."

I knew that.

As another one pierced the night, I slid my knife back into its sheath, refusing to meet his gaze. Yondus demanded a ridiculous amount of space when it came time to mate. No other critters wanted to get caught between their squirming bodies as they turned the forest floor into a furry ball of lust.

"Pick up the pace, everyone," I said, marching faster. "The yondus can't be that far from us."

As if they'd heard me, hundreds of them started howling, circling us somewhere in the dark. Their high-pitched notes of horniness left me shaken, and I snapped

To Have and to Lose

out my wings to launch into the air. I just flapped them when a massive fucking yondu burst out of the underbrush in front of us.

It careened straight towards me, its powerful legs an orange and black blur beneath it. The one I'd captured for Jace all those years ago had been a fraction of this one's size. Its green eyes fastening on me, it howled its mating call and stood up on its back legs. Its penis, red and angry, shot out in front of it, and it had to lean back so it didn't topple over.

A scream stuck in my throat, I jumped into the air. The others launched beside me, and we'd just barely missed being grabbed by its furry hands.

Dozens of them scrambled across the forest floor, swinging their dicks as they found partners in the growing ball of fur beneath us. The giant yondus, a more vicious type than their smaller brethren, rolled across the forest floor as we flew over them. Occasionally, a paw swiped up to grab at us, but we couldn't fly much higher without risking getting spotted by our enemies.

Banking left and right, we flew to the edge of the orgy. And then well beyond. Landing, I breathed heavily. My eyes found Jace's and then the other two's. We all tried to fight it, but I was the first to giggle, and after that, no one could help themselves.

"They're so freaking unnatural," Tory wheezed as she held her hands in front of her as if gripping a very large penis. Swinging her hips back and forth, she howled in between her pathetic attempt to stay silent.

Evangeline snorted, a hand over her lips as she shook her head. "One *touched* me." Balancing on her wooden limb, she shook out her leg. "It makes me want to cut this off."

I nearly died as my eyes landed on the jet of white cum

painting her leather. Doubling over, I held my stomach and pressed the back of a fist to my mouth. Tears in my eyes, I struggled to stay as quiet as possible.

"You think that's bad," Jace said as he turned around, spreading his wings. His ass hung out of his trousers, his clothes ripped clean through.

Suddenly finding the power not to laugh, I stared at the pale cheeks of his ass. *Fuck...*

Evangeline and Tory quieted too, their small snickers dying completely.

Turning back around, Jace rolled his eyes. "Really?" he teased. "You can't stop objectifying me for one moment?"

Evangeline snorted, the first to recollect herself. "I bet you cut your trousers yourself. You're such an attention whore."

"I bet you *liked* the yondu doing that," I teased, my words way more breathless than I would've liked. I wondered if I could see more if he leaned over.

"Oh you know it." He winked at me, and I shook my head, trying to put out the fire raging across my cheeks. Raising a hand, I hid behind it for just a second. His grin widened.

Clearing my throat, I dropped my arm. "It'll probably be best if we just cut the flap off so it doesn't snag."

He raised a brow, his smile way too hot. "Or Evangeline can just fix it. You know, with her magic."

My teeth ground together as I looked at my friend. "Ah, yes," I said, really not wanting to continue. Despite the logic, I didn't want her anywhere near his ass. "That makes sense."

"You'll have to take them off," she said, stepping forward as she rolled her lips. "Both of them. Don't want to accidentally mend your skin to the fabric."

He glanced at me, then the other two. Shrugging, he

unzipped his trousers and started to tug them down.

My eyes widened as a *whoosh* of air escaped my lips. A low whimper came from my left. Lunging towards him, I blocked the other women's view.

"Gods!" I snapped, grabbing his arm. I turned him around and started shoving his back, above his wings, my eyes *not* on his exposed ass. "Go behind that rock and toss them over. Have some decency."

He chuckled as he let me push him behind some cover. Just as I was about to head back to the others, though, he pivoted and grabbed my arm, keeping me hidden with him. He backed me up against the rock, then leaned in, caging me in his arms, locking away my breath. "Thank you, princess," he murmured, his lips not far from mine, "for thinking about my *decency*."

His eyes dipped to my mouth before crawling back up again, holding mine. He lowered his hands. My eyes shot open wide at the soft scuffle of his clothes sliding down his legs. He stepped out of them, never once breaking gaze.

I breathed heavily, struggling to keep my eyes up. To keep my hands at my sides. But every part of me wanted to look down as I threw myself forward, closing the scant distance still between us, the distance full of heat.

If you play with fire, you're going to get burned.
And one day, you'll have to watch him die.

Silent tears filled me over that truth, dousing the flames. I cleared my throat. "You should chuck them over now."

"Yeah."

But he didn't move.

And neither did I.

We just stood there, breathing each other's air, our eyes locked on a future neither of us were strong enough to grasp. Even if we had this moment, this soft, quiet moment behind this rock, what would be the point? We'd just lose it all as soon as we left.

Everyone dies. Nothing lasts.

Leaning his head down, he pressed his forehead to mine. "One day this war will be over."

His breath tickled my lips just as his words did my heart. I wanted to believe him; that's why we were here, well behind enemy lines, but...

"*Princess*," he groaned, tilting his head to the side.

Screams erupted inside me. Tears clogged them in my throat. Nothing good would come from this. I wouldn't be able to watch him get hurt, watch him sacrifice his life for mine as his position demanded.

But as his lips lowered to mine, my heart strangled my brain, smothering its cries to push him away. Grabbing his leather, I wrenched him flush against me. My chin lifted as he cursed, and then my lips were on –

Nothing?

He'd turned at the last second, ducking his head against my neck. Breathing heavily, he dug his fingers into my wrists. Pulling my hands off him, he stepped back, a ragged exhale touching him everywhere I wanted to touch him. "Fuck, princess, don't do that."

"Me?" My jaw dropped. "You just –"

He stepped forward, yanking my hands over my head, crowding me again. Holding them high above me, he lowered his head. "You can't touch me right now." His words were strained and hoarse.

I swallowed. My chest rose between us, nowhere close to touching him, but my nipples hardened under my cuirass all the same. I wanted to arch my back and close the distance, but I didn't dare move in case he stepped away again. "Why not?" I breathed, playing too close to the fire.

"Hey, you two!" Evangeline hissed from the other side of the rock. "Finish fucking and let's go. We're on a schedule."

My eyes widening, I pulled my arms free and shoved him back. He moved easily. Bending down, he grabbed his black trousers, no boxers, and tossed them to me. I didn't look at him as I scurried back to the others. I didn't look at them either as I transferred the bundle in my arms to Evangeline.

"Fix them and let's go," I said, ignoring the fact that I'd been the one holding everyone up. As if I had done that. As if I had taken a moment when so many people were dying.

Stupid, selfish woman...
To have anything is to lose it all.

We arrived beneath Emirin's canopy roughly four hours later. Jace kept looking at me, but I ignored him. Anything between us would be pointless. Worse, if we got caught by the Vylians and they realised I – That he meant something to me... He would be tortured for years just to break me.

"We end this tonight," I said, wanting so desperately to believe it.

King Dravr was somewhere in that tree. The head of our enemy would not see the morning. And then maybe, once the Okahi and Alzans were also defeated...

I finally looked at Jace.

He nodded at me, and I glanced away.

"One day this war will be over."

"I can cloak us for an hour," Evangeline said as she

pulled out her wand. "But you can't bump into anyone. They'll still be able to feel us, hear us – and hurt us."

I nodded. She started to wave her wand at Tory when a horn blared on our left. I spun around, my eyes widening as I watched dozens of our ravens dive down from the skies.

Blasts of red magic rained down from dozens of wands as my people attacked a tree well past Emirin.

"Seqora!" I shouted as I spread my wings. Although I could not see my older sister amongst the black cloud of ravens, this attack had her name all over it. Emirin was the deepest post of the Vylian army. Anything past that was full of innocent civilians. *Children.*

"Prin–" Jace cut himself off as he flew up beside me.

"What are you doing?" Tory hissed as she and Evangeline joined us. "We're here to kill the king, not help your sister. She'll be fine."

Help? Horrified that I'd ever been betrothed to her, I drew my sword. "Save the children," I told Jace, knowing he would follow whatever order I gave. A royal guard could not disobey me.

"What?" Tory screeched. "They're Vylians! We have an opportunity to –"

"Then do it!" I snapped. "But I'm not leaving them."

Cursing, she spun around, actually heading back towards Emirin. I cursed, too, knowing that I would be whipped upon my return to Raza once Mother found out what I'd done. Tory's life was worth more than a squadron of *our* soldiers. She was damn well worth a whole city of Vylians to them, and I would be punished for putting her in danger.

But I couldn't let my sister slaughter civilians.

Tragedy in war was one thing.

This was...

To Have and to Lose

"Seqora!" Aiming for a random raven, I flew over it, then dropped down on top of it. Throwing its rider off, I pressed my heels into the bird, pulling it back from its attack. Swivelling my head around, I searched for my sister.

Children screamed as they were pulled out of their homes and slaughtered in the streets. Houses were lit on fire. The upper branches were sawed off and crashed onto those below.

"Stop!" I shouted, but no one listened to me. We were at war, and these soldiers, these *monsters* were fighting for their lives.

Jace swooped past me on another bird, grabbing a child that was just about to be executed. Another bird flew at him. An arrow was shot in his direction. He twisted, saving the Vylian and taking the hit himself.

I screamed as I aimed for my own soldier. Her eyes widened as I jumped off my raven and onto hers. Knocking her in the jaw, I shoved my sword hilt-deep into her chest and then shoved her off. She fell to the forest floor, her screams mixing with all the others.

Yanking the bird around, I looked for Jace. The child in his arms was now slumped over, blood seeping from her throat. There was no saving the Vylians.

"Seqora!" I shouted, searching for the source of this madness.

She slammed into me, her raven clawing at mine. Its beaked stabbed my chest, and I cried out as it ripped me off my bird and threw me through the air.

Jace caught me, the child now gone, and I looked up at him in horror. His jaw tight, he urged his steed upwards. It dodged the branches before bursting out into the sky. The morning sun was just starting to colour the clouds. So much beauty.

My eyes dropped to the tree below me.

So much horror.

"We can't leave them!"

"If we stay, Seqora will kill you." He turned the bird northward, away from home. "The best we can do is warn the other cities."

I clung to him as I nodded. He didn't tell me this would be a victory like Tory would've. He didn't tell me we should use this distraction to kill the king, as Seqora most definitely had planned.

Pulling myself upright, I straddled the bird. Fresh blood stained my cuirass, but this time, it was his. He'd been shot in the arm he'd caught me with. I wanted to see how bad he was hurt, but focusing on it would kill the adrenaline pumping through our bodies, keeping down the pain.

Looking behind me, I held my breath and prayed to Loki smoke didn't fill the air. The use of true fire would kill us all. The flames shot from our soldiers' wands had been a brilliant green, magical ones that died within minutes, but that didn't mean that was all she'd use.

Closing my eyes when the skies stayed clear, I turned back to face forward. The bird dived a moment later, and the cry of a horn flared to life. Soon its echo spread throughout the forest, and an army of Vylians followed us to Emirin.

We crashed onto a branch of Hare an hour later, breathing heavily, blood seeping from our various wounds. We'd barely made it out alive. Many of our people hadn't been that lucky, but they'd crossed a line accepting my sister's orders without question. I did not

To Have and to Lose

mourn them.

On shaky legs, I turned to Jace. "Someone get us a healing wand," I called out as Stevie and Richard raced over to us. I just started to reach for his arm when a raven cawed angrily above us.

Jace shoved me behind him as my sister landed. His hand went for his blade, but I grabbed his fingers before he could. Squeezing him, I held him still. To attack her was to die. He would be publicly executed; being caught by the Vylians would be a kinder fate.

Jumping down off her steed, she aimed straight for me. I shoved Jace out of the way, into Richard as she clocked me hard in the jaw.

Praying my brother held Jace back, I straightened to look at Seqora. Her lilac eyes, so similar to mine, blazed with a fury laced with madness. "When someone gives you a fucking distraction, you use it, asswipe. King Dravr could have been dead by now." She turned to glance around the crowd that had formed around us. "This war could have been won by now, but instead we'll lose thousands more of our people because of *you*."

Drawing a knife, she slammed it into my side. I gasped as I fell against her. My eyes flew to Jace, and I watched Richard choke him out. So much rage twisted his face. So much relief filled mine.

Seqora would not kill me.

She wouldn't even harm me that badly.

To do so would be to die.

A princess could not kill her sisters outside of a fairy ring before the time of accession, where we'd then fight to the death.

Sneering at me, she held me up so she could whisper in my ear. "When Mother dies, Reli, I will kill you slowly."

Grabbing her knife, she ripped it free, and I fell to my

knees, my eyes on Jace.

They flicked to Richard as I pressed my hands against my side. *Thank you for saving him.*

His lips tightened as he watched our sister walk away. She pulled herself up onto her raven, and a moment later, she was gone.

But her words, her actions, they haunted me.

Everyone who dies now is on me.

TEN

A royal guard must not hesitate to sacrifice their life.

I will not let him die for me.

— Aurelia

"What the fuck, princess?"

"What the fuck, Jace!" I screamed as he kicked open the door of my locked bathroom and stormed in. The hot water cascading over my naked, soapy body suddenly flashed cold, and I screamed again. "Did you just flush the fucking toilet!"

Jumping out from under the spray, I wiped at the suds running into my eyes. His shadow moved on the other side of the shower curtain, making me jump for a whole different reason. Intensely aware that I was naked and wet, I stayed frozen even as steam curled back up in front of me.

I wondered if he was going to come in. I wondered if I *wanted* him to come in. The blood I'd collected on me after our visit behind enemy lines was now free of my body. The wound in my side was healed. We could just be together in this little cubicle and let the water wash everything else away.

My heart aching with things I could never have, I stepped back under the spray and started wiping the suds off my skin.

"Do you want to explain to me why you were so fucking stupid?"

"Says the person that reached for a knife!" I rubbed angrily at my hair as my pulse hammered as strong as it had in front of my sister. He had almost got himself killed, yet he was calling *me* stupid?

"I'm your guard. That's my whole fucking job!"

I screamed as the water rushed cold again. "Stop flushing the fucking toilet!"

Twisting off the shower, I rolled my eyes when I heard the flush handle being slammed down over and over again. A small smile pulled at my lips despite the harsh beating of my heart. "She would've killed you," I said gruffly, turning to look at him through the curtain.

"Not if I'd killed her first."

"Oh my gods, you thickheaded idiot!" I yanked the curtain back so I could pin him with the full force of my glare so he'd know just how fucking stupid *he* was being. "And then –" I started, but he threw a pile of clothes directly at my face.

"You're not distracting me while I yell at you." The curtain screeched across the rail, he pulled it so fast.

Catching the clothes as they started to fall, I opened my mouth as I blinked dumbly. Shaking my head, I recollected myself and exhaled sharply. "Are you going to give me a towel?"

"No. You don't deserve one."

To Have and to Lose

"Well, I'm not getting dressed while wet."

"Yes, you are."

"No, I'm not."

He growled. The cupboard in the bathroom slammed open. Then a towel was thrown over the railing. It landed on my head, and I shuffled my clothes around as I dried myself.

Grumbles sounded from the other side, a low constant hum as he no doubt cursed me under his breath. Shivers running up my arms and legs, I ignored the heat bridging between us. The shower curtain was a pathetic dam.

Mostly dried, I let the towel drop to my feet as I searched through the bundle of clothes he'd thrown at me. At the sight of my underwear, I froze. He'd gone through my drawers! Oh gods, what if he'd found 'Mof'.

What if? I screamed internally. There was no 'what if'. Magically Operated Fuckboy wasn't exactly hidden. It was just plopped in there with my panties and bras – a drawer he'd clearly rifled through.

"Did you..." I squeaked. "It isn't mine," I said, then instantly winced, wondering how the heck I was going to lie my way out of that. Whose else's could it possibly be given no one entered my private rooms except for him and Dickie? "It's my brother's!" I blurted, flames of Tartarus bursting across my cheeks. I was clearly going there when I died.

A weird noise came from the other side of the curtain – half growl, half groan.

I waited, my heart beating hard as I wondered if he bought it.

Each word seemingly pulled from him by a pair of pliers, he said, "Why would he keep it in *your* drawer then?"

My mouth opened and closed multiple times. "Because

he has a fetish?" I winced so hard I felt I was going to be sick. Yep. I was definitely going to the worst level of Niflhel.

That weird noise came again, though this time it sounded more strained. More...something. "Are you dressed yet?" he rasped finally.

"No."

"*Fuck, princess.*" He groaned this time. A clear fucking groan that made me really want to pull the shower curtain back and step out as I was.

But Jace joked and flirted with everyone, and the fear that what we had...what I *hoped* we had... I didn't want to face the truth of that. Regardless of the outcome, I would only be hurt. *A fairy queen eliminates her weaknesses...*

Tucking the other clothes under my arm, I slipped on my underwear and then my bra. Ignoring the fact that his hands had been on them, ignoring the thoughts of having him touch them now while they were on me, I finished getting dressed. I pulled the curtain back and immediately sucked in a sharp breath.

He was staring at me, so hungrily and feral I nearly stepped back and turned on the cold tap.

"Jace?"

His eyes caressed my body, burning a path straight down to the underwear he'd chosen for me.

And then they came back up, so slow and pained I couldn't help but pant.

"Fuck, princess, don't do that."

"Do what?" I breathed, wishing so fucking hard I had the strength to step out of the shower and into his arms.

His face twisted, raw and primal for just a moment. Then he blinked, and his emotions were gone, hidden under a mask of irritation. "Don't shove me out of the way when you're in danger."

To Have and to Lose

He took a step forward, and I was acutely aware that I didn't have any room to retreat.

"She would've killed you."

His arm lifted, then dropped. I could see his fingers flexing in my peripheral, but my attention was solely on his eyes. On his beautiful teal eyes that warred with irritation, fear, and hunger. He stepped closer, and I lifted my chin to hold his gaze.

His breath tickling my lips, he murmured, "It is my duty to die for you, princess."

His gaze dropped to my lips.

I sucked in a breath.

The air froze in my lungs, unmoving.

So still.

My heart pounded. My eyes fluttered shut.

I leaned up on my toes, wanting so badly just to have this one. This one moment just for me...

But only the air kissed my lips.

And when I opened my eyes, he was gone.

Alone in the bathroom, I wrapped my arms around my stomach and told myself his rejection was for the best.

Nothing good can come from us...
Nothing good at all.

ELEVEN

A fairy princess must eliminate all her weaknesses.

Jace will always be mine.

- Aurelia

Falling back against the wet shower wall, I closed my eyes as my throat worked to swallow down my frustration, pain, and the utter ache in my heart. Jace and I... He was a future I could never have, not in this life. Not when I was a princess and he was my guard. If anything ever happened between us, our enemies would take one look at me and know I would trade myself to get him back.

It's my duty to die for you, princess.

And it was my duty to let him. For my people.

But maybe...

Tears burning my eyes, I forced them open, forced those thoughts down, forced myself to stay rooted in a world I could not escape. The wet shower surrounded me,

To Have and to Lose

and just beyond the bathroom's door was a half-destroyed, crumbling home whose occupants had died for this kingdom.

I had to honour their sacrifice.

A princess wed to strengthen her kingdom.

A princess did not love.

A princess eliminated all her weaknesses, like Seqora had her childhood best friend.

Rubbing a hand down my face, I looked at my reflection in the mirror. Condensation clung to it, making it hazy, but the pain in my eyes, the *weakness* was as clear as the stars on a cloudless sky.

You're a princess, Aurelia. Start fucking acting like it.

Glancing away, I took a deep shuddering breath.

Held it against the ache of my lungs.

Until the tears inside me finally burned away.

Exhaling slowly, I stepped out of the shower.

I found my brother waiting for me in the living room, leaning against the back of the sofa, his arms crossed, his eyes serious and fierce.

"Thank you for knocking Jace out," I said, only the smallest crack to my voice.

He stared at me in silence for a moment before everything about him sagged – his shoulders, his chest, his eyes.

Gods, he looks so tired.

He exhaled sharply, then lifted his gaze back up. "Seqora is out for blood," he said.

I chuckled softly as I waved at my healed side. "Really? Because that was not the impression I got from her at all."

"From Evangeline and Tory when they get back," Richard said flatly, sending a spike of panic straight into my heart, "for not stopping you."

I rushed for the door, my wings starting to spread, but

he stepped in front of me and grabbed my arm.

"If you challenge her in this, she will kill Evangeline to punish you."

I didn't want to believe him. I didn't want to be helpless in this, but the honesty in his words struck me to my bones. My shoulders shaking, I rasped, "What is she going to do to them?"

"She won't break them."

But she would fucking try, especially with Evangeline. The two were betrothed to combine our families, love having no place in our world, and Seqora would see this as an absolute betrayal.

"*Tell me*," I demanded.

All emotion fled from his eyes, and my heart was pierced by a thousand splinters. Richard could shut himself off in a way I never could, and in this moment, I hated him for that ability.

Evangeline and Tory were our *friends*.

"She's prepping to skin them."

I staggered back, a broken rasp leaving me.

"They will heal," he said without feeling. "She won't risk their deaths."

I shook my head, horror muting me. But then one thought screamed so loudly, I wanted to drop to my knees under its torment. "What about Jace?" A rasped broken sentence I barely managed to utter.

But the pain in my eyes as I looked at my brother spoke the question clearly.

"He cannot defy you," he said softly. "She has no right to punish him."

And gods, I hated that I felt relief in this moment, when Tory and Evangeline would still suffer because of me. As nobles, it was their duty to rebel against a royal's leadership should they lead us into ruin.

To Have and to Lose

As we held each other's gazes –tears in mine, nothing in his– broken laughter ruptured the air outside. A shudder shot through me, and I fell forward against my brother's chest, wrapping him in my arms.

Evangeline never screamed, but her laughter was somehow worse.

Richard squeezed me tightly for a second, then grabbed my arms and forced them apart. I knew the words he was about to say, knew the duty that was expected of me.

Knew the respect my friends would want.

"You must watch," he said softly, tilting my chin up.

I wanted to shake my head. I wanted to beg him not to make me go.

But I was a fairy princess.

And we did not show any weaknesses.

"You look like shit," Evangeline said as she sat up in bed. Her new skin looked raw and tight. Seqora had ordered the two of them to be healed immediately after their torture given their importance in battle, but the healer, like all of us, was only young. She had only been able to heal so much.

Tory laid in the cot beside Evangeline, her skin looking a more natural tan, having been treated first, before the healer had run out of magic. Her magical tattoos had stayed on her muscles and were still as prominent and powerful as they'd always been. Richard had been ordered away by Seqora on some miniscule mission after she'd finished punishing them. He was a brilliant tactician, but to her, he was just 'a boy' who had no place in command. And Jace...

Jace stood guard at the door, his presence at my back

palpable, his cocky smile as I'd entered painful. Not a trace of regret had been in his eyes, no hope for a future that could never be.

Forcing out a laugh, I focused on my two friends. They had suffered so much for me. "At least I don't smell like it," I teased, the humour helping us all cope.

Tory wrinkled her nose. "Sorry to tell you this, Aurelia, but you fucking stink."

"Hey, I just had a shower." My hair was still wet. Seqora hadn't dragged out their torture, thank gods, and she was horrifyingly adept at skinning.

Raising an arm over her head, Tory said, "Yeah, but that has nothing on new skin smell." She turned her head into her armpit, sniffed deeply, and grinned. "Mmm."

Pretending to hold up a mirror, Evangeline turned her head back and forth. "Oh my gods, my pores haven't been this clear for *years,*" she cooed.

"Someone needs to add skinning to a spa day."

"*Yes!*"

A chuckle escaped me as I shook my head, the tension in my shoulders finally easing. "There's something wrong with you two."

They glanced at each other, a wicked smirk in each of their eyes. Turning to me as one, they said in unison, "Yeah, we know you."

It was a joke we all made about each other whenever the situation arose, but this time it dug a little deeper. It was because of me that they were lying in these cots.

My smile flickered.

My throat pulled tight.

I started to say something, but Evangeline groaned, "Ugh, she has that look on her face, Tory. The chick's about to *monologue.*"

"*Nooo.* I thought our torture was over." She flopped

back into bed dramatically, the back of her hand pressing against her forehead. "But it's only just begun."

Jace's presence appeared right behind me, and his hand touched the small of my back. Electrifying and agonising.

I sucked in a breath, my attention diverted away from my two idiot friends. I turned my head to glance at him, but his eyes were on Evangeline. "Give her a break, you two. She's traumatised over realising her skin will never smell as lovely as yours."

"Hey!" I elbowed him hard in the stomach.

He grunted on a chuckle as he turned his head towards me. The brilliance of his smile rooted me, and before I could think of anything with substance, he leaned his nose into my neck.

His breath kissed my skin, and if I wasn't so fucking frozen, I would've swooned into him.

Ugh, swooned, *Aurelia?*

But even as that thought filled me, gods, I wanted to *swoon.*

"Yep," he murmured, his lips sending shivers across my skin, zinging straight to my – "You have that old skin smell."

Evangeline and Tory laughed as I sputtered. Shoving him away from me, I glared at the lot of them. "You are all deranged."

"But alive," Evangeline said softly, holding my gaze. "With no regrets."

"Ugh, are we really doing this?" Tory moaned. "Talking about our *feelings.* Fine." Sitting up, she looked at me too. "You're a nobhead who should have killed King Dravr while his guards were distracted. We almost did it, and if Jace was there, we would've. We could've dealt a good blow to the Vylians. And instead, you threw a hissy fit about dead people not even on our side."

"They were kids, Tory," Jace said.

She glanced at him. "That will become adults who kill us."

My chest tightened over the harsh proclamation of her words. But I'd expected this from her – our differing opinions on the Vylians was an old argument we often clashed over.

"I'm sorry I let you down and caused you to get skinned," I said around the lump in my throat, but I wasn't sorry for what I'd done. It had been the right thing to do.

Her different coloured eyes back on me, she exhaled hard, then opened her mouth.

But before she could say anything, Evangeline cut in, "Oh, she's just pissy because King Dravr's her *lifemate*."

"What?" My head snapped to her, but my mouth dropped to the floor instead. A lifemate was the literal other half of one's soul, pulled apart by the gods upon our creation. Both halves were flung across the Seven Planes, left to find each other, most never doing so. I had never found mine.

Perhaps Jace is holding out for his...

My lungs shrivelled, but I shoved such thoughts down. It didn't matter *why* he didn't return my feelings. Even if he did return them, I was a fairy princess. My life was not my own.

"He is not," Tory bit out, scowling at her friend.

"Uhh, the aura around you two snapped *crazy* hot." Unlike the rest of us, Evangeline's magic allowed her to glimpse into our very souls. "How do you think we got out of there alive? He ordered his guards to not give chase."

"He chased us himself!" she said, throwing her arms about.

"Yeah, to make sure you got out alive." A smug grin

To Have and to Lose

curled her lips.

"I tried to stab him."

"But you didn't."

"Because he was so fast!"

"And hot."

"Exactly!" Her eyes widened in horrified realisation. "No!" she sputtered.

As the three of us laughed, I wondered if Evangeline was telling the truth or lying just to disperse the tension that had started to build. She was always looking out for us like that. I smiled at her softly, and she caught my eye with a smirk.

I love you.

Three words she would never utter aloud in this wretched world of ours but ones I felt all the same.

I love you too.

My eyes skirted to Tory.

And you.

They landed on Jace and held.

My throat worked, blocked by three words I would never get to say.

One year.

One more year of going back and forth with the Vylians and nothing changed. Each fight was the same. Some we lost. Some we won. Some we won, but they felt like a loss. And now, here we were: right back where we'd been years ago – fighting to take back Hare.

The only difference was the new faces.

And my sister had found the bees.

TWELVE

A ruler who wishes to negotiate is weak. That is when you should strike the hardest.

What is so weak about peace?

- Aurnelia

The bees were killing more of us than the Vylians had in the last five years. Tears in my eyes, I watched my people get slaughtered. Who the eighty thousand bees didn't poison with their stingers, they killed in an explosion. We were dying by the hundreds. By the thousands. More?

As one flew straight at me, I threw a knife into the explosive wards tattooed on its face. Just as it detonated, I banked to the right, looking for my next target.

King Dravr and Seqora were fighting somewhere, lost in the smoke filling the trees. His skills were legendary enough to make me hope he would kill her. That he would stop her madness before it spread further than this. In the last year, she'd lost all sight of her humanity, doing

To Have and to Lose

whatever it took, offering whatever sacrifices it required to deal a blow to our enemies. She had remembered to spell the bees to not explode with true fire, but how long would it be until she forgot?

Or gods, deliberately didn't?

Fire would kill us all.

"Aurelia!"

Jace tackled me from the back, his arms wrapping around me as the whistle of an arrow cut somewhere beside us. My eyes burning from the smoke, I tried to peer around in the darkness for the archer, but there was too much chaos. Screams and the clash of weapons were drowned out by the loud drum of the insects' wings. Explosions erupted through the smog, followed by flashes of strong light in the otherwise encroaching darkness. Arrows and blasts of magic whizzed in every direction as people attacked blindly. Friends hit friends as much as foes. Afraid of doing the same, I was keeping my arrows until I could see a Vylian's uniform.

"I don't see them!" I shouted over the rush of the wind as we tumbled through the air.

His wings spread out, catching us right before we hit a branch. Lowering me to the ground, he kept his eyes up, searching the darkness. With a snap of his arm, he tossed a knife through the smog. A second later, a Vylian fell with it embedded in his heart, his bow clattering down beside him.

Shoving Jace out of the way, I quickly nocked an arrow and let it fly. Another one was ready before the first hit its target. As Jace guarded my back, we fought against the dozen or so Vylians suddenly surrounding us.

Adrenaline rushed through my veins as I rotated the arrow flush against the bow and ran my fingers down the runes etched into the wood of the lower limb. Evangeline had spelled it for me last year, once she'd learned such magic. As the wood of the two warped together and twisted into the metal of a sword, I swivelled it in my hands, holding it in front of me. Three soldiers charged me.

The boy on the left stumbled forward, his eyes widening as he hit his knees before collapsing onto his face. Leaping over his body, Evangeline hit the branch with her shoulder and rolled towards Jace and I as she shot a blast of magic into the Vylian on the right. Blood erupted out of his neck, a phallus-shaped stick flying through his throat. It appeared in her hand as she rolled to her feet, and she smirked at me as she lifted it. "A souvenir for Testes."

Testes was the Vylian whose balls she kept growing and whose dick she kept shrinking. I felt bad for not knowing his actual name at this point given the years we'd known him, but Testes just fit him so well.

"He's going to kill you if you give that to him."

She grinned, not bothered in the slightest. As skilled of a fighter as Testes was, double swords were shit against magic.

Quick movement to my right had me lifting my blade as Evangeline said something I didn't catch. The third Vylian's sword clashed against mine, both raised high as he'd aimed for my head. Using his momentum and power against him, I stepped back, forcing him to stumble through, before darting to the side. As his sword finished its arc, cutting down to the floor, I sliced open his unprotected back. Then on the return, I lobbed off his head.

A shimmering shield of blue light shot up in front of me a second before a blast of magic exploded across it. Red tendrils wrapped around the shield, reaching for me as Evangeline grunted beside me.

"Go!" she screamed as she stepped in front of me, her wand glowing with an intense light that looked like it might explode.

Despite wanting to stay and help, I turned to find Jace. Magic needed to be fought with magic. I would only get in her way.

As laughter trickled out behind me, I swung my sword at a Vylian trying to kill Jace. She fell, an arc of blood spraying out from her back. As she tumbled onto her side, I saw a throwing knife already embedded in her front.

"Trying to steal my kills, princess?" Jace teased as he cut another Vylian's throat, then shoved him off the branch. The rats and crows would tear them to pieces, making sure they couldn't be resurrected to fight again, necromancy requiring a mostly healthy and intact body to work.

"Watch out!" I screamed as a bee aimed straight for us, flying over the Vylians rushing towards us. Our enemies ducked, then spread their wings and fled. I wanted to do the same, but that would leave Evangeline's back wide open.

Grabbing a knife from my belt, I stepped to the side, lining myself up with it. The world stilling, I tossed the blade at the bee charging, hoping to detonate the explosive runes before it reached us.

But I was too late.

It was too close.

As the bee exploded in a blast of magic, my hair flew back and my weight started to lift off my feet. Jumping in front of me, Jace wrapped me in his arms. He grunted as he took the full force of energy on his back, his teeth gritting in a flash of pain. His grip loosened around me. The metallic tang of blood filled my nostrils, smothering the cry in my lungs. Holding my gaze, a soft smile forced onto his lips, Jace's eyes flickered.

No!

Refusing to let death take him, I held onto him tight.

Pumping my wings, I carried us away from the bloodbath of battle. I weaved through the branches of the tree. My people were dying around me, Evangeline was all on her own, and here I was fleeing to save just one man.

But it wasn't *just* one man.

It was Jace.

Stupid. Annoying. Jace.

"Don't you die on me," I half-commanded, half-begged, my heart in my throat, flying fast.

But just as we landed on another tree, he looked up and smiled, no flash of pain in his beautiful eyes. "Told you you'd be upset if I died."

Clenching my teeth, I shoved him off the branch.

The fucker was more than fine.

For now.

But I was *so* going to kill him after this.

Shaping my pain into rage, I flew back into battle behind him, hoping Evangeline was still alive.

Though I knew she would've won against the other witch as Jace wouldn't have let me fly away otherwise (the blood I'd smelled had probably been the enemy's), there were hundreds of Vylians and thousands of bees still flying around.

Hopefully Richard and Tory are alive somewhere too.

I'm going to fucking kill him.

We suffered the biggest loss we'd had in the last five years and all because I'd wanted to save the bees. I was

To Have and to Lose

supposed to protect my people, and I had killed so many...

My chest ached as I remembered how Jace's arms had slackened around me. He could've died today *because of me*. Standing in my new temporary home, a wand shop mostly crumbled and missing half its roof, I felt that pain all over again. "I'm going to kill him."

But it wasn't said as angrily as it had been. It was laced in an ache I couldn't run away from.

Not anymore.

Not when I'd believed I was going to lose him.

"You daydreaming about Jace?" Richard's voice drifted in from the other side of the rubble. He'd been bloodied and bruised but alive, as was Tory. Standing in the moonlight, my brother looked at me, his violet eyes seeing too much.

"What are you doing here?" I snapped, not feeling like being teased right now. For the hundredth time, I regretted breaking down last year and telling Richard I wanted to marry Jace. After Seqora had captured the children of Vylian commanders and then executed them on the front lines before battle, I hadn't been able to handle the sight of all their small bodies. When Jace had tried to save those she'd accidentally only wounded, I'd known then that he was the kind of person I wanted to marry. Not some necromancer who had no guilt over reviving fairies just to watch them die all over again.

But transitioning from friends to lovers would eventually wreck me.

Because one day he would be gone.

Just like Brooke was.

Just like Stevie...

She'd fallen out of bed and onto a snake sleeping beneath the tree. The snake had not stayed sleeping like she had.

92

"I came to see if you were okay," Richard said softly, all humour gone. "I saw you with that Vylian after battle."

My chest ached for an entirely different reason. "You mean that *boy*." He'd been young, too young to have gone through his ascension, a magical puberty that allowed his body to heal itself. He would've died without me healing his wounds with a pre-made wand, spelled for anyone to be able to use them.

Would've died without Jace protecting him from our soldiers after.

Instead, he'd lived long enough to kill seven of our people, having copied the explosive ward on the bees onto his own chest.

Tears burning my eyes, I looked away. "It's all so fucking *pointless*. We're just killing each other generation after generation and *nothing changes*. Don't you wish it was different? Peaceful? Like with the brownies?" Hugging my waist, I stepped over the rubble and looked at the branches above. I couldn't see the stars from beneath the foliage, couldn't see the prospect of peace under our mindless wars.

We'd been fighting with the Vylians for millennia. A civil war that had long got out of hand, progressing into a furious slaughter of revenge, a constant spew of 'You killed my brother!', 'my sister', 'my child', 'my mum'...

Stepping beside me, Richard wrapped an arm around my waist, beneath my softly glowing wings. "I would never want to be like a brownie," he said. "Before you arrived, Seqora used some as magic fodder. I thought it would be nice not hearing any screams for a change, but watching them all get slaughtered while laughing happily... It's too fucking eerie. There's something not right with them."

"I didn't mean it like that..."

To Have and to Lose

He squeezed my waist. "Maybe when you're queen, *kultara*, you can actually work towards peace. But for now, you have to stay strong."

I stepped away from him, gesticulating in desperation. "What is *weak* about wanting peace? Maybe if someone actually *talked* to King Dravr, we could end this stupid war."

And then kids wouldn't have to die. *Jace* wouldn't have to die. Nor would Richard or Evangeline or Tory.

Or stupid fucking *Jace*.

Shaking out my hands, I started to pace. "What if I tried to talk to him? We could meet somewhere neutral and –"

"He'd kill you."

"You don't know that." *Or maybe, if Tory is really his lifemate –*

"Yes, I do."

"No, you –"

"Yes," he cut in firmly. Waiting until I looked into his eyes, he repeated, "I do. I tried. Against Seqora's orders, I tried, and I nearly got her killed. I *did* get three dozen fairies killed as they came to rescue me. Upon our return, Queen Helena whipped me for leaving my post. But Seqora... Mother put her in charge of killing all the prisoners of war. Of attacking the civilian cities that would give us the best advantage." His eyes flicked away. His words softened. "She lost the last of her humanity because of *me*."

Pain laced through my heart. "But you're just a prince. Maybe if he spoke to a princess..."

He closed his eyes briefly, then stepped towards me. "We'll get peace when we win this. You can see to that when you're queen."

I looked away, unable to voice the fact that I didn't

want the job. I didn't have the heart to send more children to die for a war I didn't even believe in. To have people suffer the pain I had over almost losing Jace. "We all know I cannot defeat Seqora," I said instead.

Grabbing my shoulders, his fingers dug into my flesh. "You have to, *kultara*. Seqora will see us all dead."

I pulled away, not wanting to believe him, but in my heart I knew it was true.

If only King Dravr killed her.

THIRTEEN

A queen weds for the good of her kingdom.

Jace Monningtan...
— *Aurelia*

"Princess."

Jerked out of sleep, I came up swinging. His hands grabbed both my arms, so not one of them knocked him in his pretty face. A pity. Jace deserved that and more after scaring me today.

Opening my eyes, I stared at him in the darkness of the night. "What are you doing here?" My words came out soft rather than with the underlining of steel I'd meant to use. With him, the screams of my people didn't sound so loud.

Guilt stabbed me sharp and deep.

I did not deserve happiness when my people were suffering *because of me.*

His fingers loosened around me, then trailed a hundred

goosebumps up to my elbows, quieting my agonising thoughts. "I can't stop thinking about that scream you made."

My chest squeezed as I remembered it too. The agony. The terror that I was going to lose him.

Narrowing my eyes on him, holding back the tears, I punched him in the stomach. He grunted, but the blow hadn't been heavy, our positions not allowing for much and the pain inside me making my muscles weak. "I'd thought..."

Shuddering beneath his touch and that pain, I wetted my lips.

"Fuck, princess, don't do that," he breathed, his face twisting as if there was something he wanted just out of reach. His eyes lowered, snaring the air in my lungs.

I punched him again, harder this time. "Then don't *scare* me like that. That wasn't a funny joke."

"I know."

"Then why'd you –"

"I just needed to get you away from there for a moment."

"Evangeline could've *died*."

"You moved into the way of the blast." His eyes swarmed with more words I couldn't decipher. But there was something in them that caused me to shiver. Or perhaps that was just his close proximity.

The desire to wrap him in my arms and make sure he was really alive.

Really okay.

My throat working, I wetted my lips again.

"*Fuck, princess*. I said don't do that." Those silent words strengthened, heard somewhere inside of me, making my heart pound with their loudness.

"Do *what?*" Whatever I'd done, I wanted to do it again.

To Have and to Lose

I wanted him to keep looking at me like this...
Like he most likely had at Josie all those years ago. The thought came unbidden – a pathetic attempt to keep hold of my sanity, perhaps.

A smile graced his lips. "That's more like it, princess."

He blooped my nose.

I turned my head, my scowl deepening. Why did he always have to ruin everything?

"Did you really think I was going to die?" he asked, rolling off me just to lie down beside me, resting on his side, his head propped up on one hand.

I rolled to face him. Gods, he was close.

My eyes dipped to his lips before I recalled his question. Recalled the panic he'd caused.

Fighting back the pain, the thoughts I'd had of life without him, I changed the subject. I was too raw after battle to dive headfirst into more agony. "Did you know I was under the bed?"

"When?"

My jaw clenched. "When you were with *Josie.*"

He smiled, and gods, I wanted to wipe that smirk off his face.

"As soon as I walked into the room, I knew you were in there."

"How?"

He leaned in, way too close. My breath catching, I froze, but every particle of myself was aware. Of his presence. Of his proximity. Of his nose as it pressed against my neck. My fingers balled into a fist just so I didn't reach for him and pull him closer.

"I could smell you," he murmured.

It took me a second to register his words. "You did not."

"I swear to Zeus I could." He inhaled deeply. On his exhale, my eyes couldn't help but drift close, basking in the warmth of his breath. "You smell sweet. Fucking –" He groaned low and deep. "*Good.*"

"I thought I smelled like old sk–" I arched my neck as his lips softly brushed my skin. A shudder raced through me, following the trails of electricity awakening the parts of me I'd been desperate to keep asleep after his rejection a year ago. Pots and pans banging inside of me, not letting one part of me stay in slumber, I threaded my fingers through his hair.

His lips pressed more firmly against my skin.

A groan reverberated against the outside of my throat as he shifted on the bed, the mattress moving me into a dip closer to his body.

My fingers tightened as the electricity set every nerve on fire, and my lips parted to release the rush of energy fully consuming me.

I held him to me, desperate for the comfort of his touch, for the creation of that one little moment I'd wanted a year ago.

His lips trailed up the arch of my neck, and I started to turn to face him, to finally *have* him when a thought blared through the haze of my desire.

A scowl forming, I tightened my grip on his hair until he winced. "And you still had sex with Josie? That's so gross."

Laughing, he removed my hold on him and leaned back to look me in the eyes. As teal danced before me, he ran his thumb across my hand. "I actually didn't."

I stared at him in dumb silence.

Lowering our hands between our bodies, he pressed my palm against his stomach.

My eyes widened, and my lips parted, and for a moment I glanced down, wanting to –

"I used my fingers."

To Have and to Lose

My gaze jerked up. "What?"

He shrugged. "I couldn't get hard knowing you were under us." He lowered my hand even further. My eyes dipped down again. My fingers were so sensitive, I felt as if I could detect each fine individual hair beneath his clothes. "All I could think about was kicking Josie out of my room and joining you."

My palm pressed firmer against him, guided by the rough pounding in my veins. "So why didn't you?" I breathed.

"Because Richard ordered me to get close to the Court so I'd know what they were planning."

My mouth fell open as I stilled to look at him. "Oh my gods. You were laughing at me when I told you she was probably using you."

"A little."

He moved my hand lower. Past his belly button. The V of his hips. I started to squirm. But just as my palm grazed the top of a bulge, I gasped. "Wait? So does that mean you're still a vir–"

"Aurelia!"

I jerked upright at the sound of my brother's voice. Groaning, Jace released me and ducked out of the open window, taking the blissful silence in my guilt-ridden skull with him.

A second later, my brother rushed to my side and yanked me out of bed. "I have to get you out of here."

I went with him, instinct kicking in. In the last five years, I'd learned to move fast and ask questions later. "What's happened?"

"Queen Helena is dying. Seqora will be coming for you."

My stomach twisted, knowing exactly what he meant to do. Richard was going to hurt her before we fought in the ring so I would have an advantage. And then I would be queen. I'd be the one ordering these people to sacrifice themselves for nothing.

"No." Digging my heels in, I ripped my arm free. *I can't.*

So many faces assaulted me. Brooke's. Stevie's. The little Vylian boy's. The seven wounded soldiers he'd killed. That *I* had killed through my actions.

"*Aurelia.*" Turning, Richard grabbed both my hands. "You cannot allow her to be queen."

"I cannot lead them either!" Jerking away from him, I wrapped my arms around my waist, the truth hitting me as hard as it was him, robbing me of the strength I pretended to have. "The Court is right. I am *weak*. Every order I give ends in so many of our people dead. I lost forty-seven saving twenty-three fairies in Hare. A hundred and sixteen saving our mother, who called Brooke a *whore* after she'd given her life... I lost four hundred at Eyr. Two thousand at Ryz. Over twenty due to the thousands of bees I didn't just kill." Swiping at the tears on my face, I shook my head. "I would be no better of a ruler than Seqora."

"Yes, you will."

"No, I won't!" Because I was too soft. Because my visions of peace, of negotiating, of saving lives would only end in more bloodshed. I was not the queen they needed right now. Every choice I'd made in the last five years had been *wrong*. Richard had questioned me every single time, but I hadn't listened. And I would never be able to listen because I truly believed you could not win peace with war. I would get them killed over and over and over again, every time hopeful that I could save everyone. That I could end this war, when the truth was –

I stopped. Lifting my eyes, I looked at him. The

screams of guilt faded just slightly under the onslaught of realisation. "You're the ruler our people need," I breathed.

"Aurelia –"

I shook my head, cutting him off. My heart pounding, my skull quieting, I rasped, "You're a brilliant tactician. Our soldiers respect you."

"The Court will not appoint me," he said, his words strained, and I knew he was grasping. I knew he had already come to the same conclusion I just did.

"They will if Seqora and I are both dead," I said softly. "If you challenge her in the fairy ring and win."

FOURTEEN

The line of succession goes to the daughter who manages to exit the fairy ring.

I hate this fucking world.

— Aurelia

"Aurelia, *please*, what you are asking me to do..."

I shook my head, knowing this was the only option our fucked up world allowed. Our people were not ready for peace. They didn't even like me healing Vylian *civilians* because they could bear children who would then slaughter our descendants. We were not ready for peace despite how much I wished we were.

"Promise me when you're king –"

"Aurelia."

"*Promise* me, Dickie, that when our people are ready, you will strive for peace."

His eyes glistened as he shook his head. "You are our rightful queen. You can lead us –"

"I will lead us to death or enslavement and you know

it."

"Jace and I can advise you. Together, we can –"

"You've been advising me these last five years, Dick!" I pressed my palms against my eyes, my chest heaving. It was my duty to do what was best for my people, and this was the only way I could. The other decisions they needed me to make, I could not make them. I *had not* been able to make them. "Please, Dickie. You said it yourself. Seqora cannot be queen."

"But you *can*."

"Even if I was stronger or faster than our sister, I cannot kill her in a fairy ring. Her soul will be trapped there forever, never allowed to reincarnate." A true tactician knew their own weaknesses, and I had never been blind to mine. "I cannot kill her there."

"Her soul will be trapped regardless."

"But *I* cannot do it. And if she leaves the fairy ring alive, she *will* be queen. It can't be me, Dickie. It can't be me who challenges her, and you can't do it if I'm still alive."

Grabbing my hands, he squeezed them, panic in his eyes. "We don't even know if the Court will allow this. There has never been a ruling king."

I shook my head. "They cannot risk a civil war." I squeezed his hands. "You *are* a Morningstar. They will appoint you king."

"*Aurelia*." A pained cry. A broken desperate plea.

Taking a deep breath, I removed my hands from his and cupped his face. There was no other way to save our people. Drawing on all the strength I had, I steeled my voice into one of regal command even as tears burned in my heart. "I am ordering you, brother, as your princess, to kill me and stop Seqora."

Tears coated my fingers, pooled beneath my palms as

he stared at me in silence. Lifting a hand, he gripped my fingers hard.

And then the future king of Raza nodded.

Forcing a smile, I tried not to think about the future I would lose.

Jace Morningstar...

FIFTEEN

Brownies' peaceful, happiness-sex cult ideology makes them great fodder...

Why does everything have to come back to war and death?

— Aurelia

The plan was simple. Richard, Nicholas, and I would go away together while Seqora and all the royal guards stayed with our dying mother. Unwatched, Richard would kill me and then claim I died of cancer in my brain. Said it would explain my 'unnatural humanity'.

As we landed in the abandoned castle that would be my final resting place, I tried to ignore the shivers running across my skin. I was eighteen, older than a lot of our people when they died. And my death would be a lot more dignified than the original occupants of this city.

They'd been overrun by giant yondus in heat – some idiot having covered himself in their musk to taunt them on top of the branches, thinking they couldn't climb trees. The Fuck-orgy Massacre had been so disturbing, the city had been turned into a ghost town overnight. Those who'd managed to flee had never gone back to collect their belongings – mostly because they'd committed suicide after seeing what they'd seen.

Landing beside me, Nicholas buzzed with excitement, his wings flickering quickly behind him, his face split into a wide grin of ignorance. "Can we go into Brownston?" he asked, nearly hopping from foot to foot as he glanced down at the festivities happening in the meadow below us.

The brownies were always having some party or another. How they hadn't celebrated themselves into death or a broken economy was beyond me. How they hadn't been fucked by yondus in both senses of the word was an even greater mystery, but yondus, for some reason, gave them a wide berth. I liked to think it was because the brownies were way too sex-obsessed even for them.

A giggle pulling at my cheeks, I grabbed my brother in a headlock and rubbed my knuckles into his head.

"Hey! You can't do that anymore! I'm a head taller than you now!" He tried to squirm away, but I kicked out one of his legs, dropping him to his knees. "Hey!"

Laughing, I released him by shoving him off the branch and then flew down after him. Richard darted below us, ready to catch his brother should he not recover in time, but I wasn't worried. We'd been shoving each other off branches since before we could fly – much to the annoyance of our guards – and not one of us had died yet.

Well, Henry, the youngest of us, had died, but really, he had never been going to live long anyway. He'd had a bad heart, and I was ninety-nine percent certain he'd died of that rather than because he'd splattered all over the ground after Seqora had pushed him.

To Have and to Lose

"I'm going to get you back for that!" Nicholas screamed as he finally righted himself, his wings flapping into a near blur. Angling for me, he shot up, a troublesome grin on his face.

Laughing, I twisted to the side right as he neared, and he shot past me with a curse. He swung around to chase me, and I flew behind Richard, putting him between us.

"Hey!" Dickie protested, trying to outfly me. He was faster and more agile than me under most circumstances, so when he struggled to keep up, I knew he was weighed down by the reason why we were here. Nicholas was blissfully ignorant, though, and wanting it to stay that way, I banked in to jab Richard in the ribs. "Smile, Dickie," I breathed before shooting off in front of him.

I barely made it a full length of my body before he grabbed my ankle and yanked. I yelped as he flung me behind him, right at an advancing Nicholas. Grabbing me, my youngest brother manoeuvred me into a headlock and rubbed my head hard.

His chest rumbling against me in laughter, I smiled and only half-heartedly tried to get away. I'd missed him these last five years and had a whole lifetime to cram into one week.

As soon as we landed in Brownston, he released me and I turned to take in his smile.

"Right," Richard said with barely concealed contempt as he looked around the place. "What should we scar ourselves with seeing first?"

Rolling my eyes, I slugged him in the shoulder. "Brownie life isn't that bad." Walking towards the sound of music, I led them to what looked to be a big celebration.

Crowded around a stage, hundreds of brownies watched a pantomime being played out with over a dozen brownie-sized puppets of various ages.

"What are they doing?" Nicholas asked as he stopped beside me, hovering high enough off the ground to actually see the stage.

My brow furrowed as I watched the line of puppets near what honestly looked like a massive vagina.

"I don't..."

The labia of the vagina suddenly spread open and sucked them all in. My eyes widened as shouts of joy rose around us, including from the little kids.

"What the fuck?"

"That's my family!" a little kid screamed, hopping up and down in laughter, her pale blue hair bouncing in high pigtails.

"You mean puppets of your family, right?" Nicholas asked her, but horror descended on me long before she opened her mouth.

"Well, they're puppets now!" she giggled. "They got sucked into an ogre's vagina during one of our orgies. Arienna, that's my sister, thinks they died by drowning. But I think they were squashed to death by a dick."

My eyes landed back on the 'puppets', their grotesque faces in various degrees of decay. I jerked back. "Oh my gods."

Richard looked at me smugly. "You were saying?"

"Do you want to take some photos with them?" the little girl asked. "Uncle Bobby has all his parts still, so you can –"

Shuddering, I launched into the air and flew back to the comforting sight of the Fuck-orgy Massacre.

"Okay, yes," I said to Richard as we landed given he was still looking at me smugly. "Brownies are fucked up." Not wanting to admit full defeat though, I quickly added, "But they have peace."

"And necrophilia," our younger brother added, not

helping.

"That's not the kind of peace you want, though, is it?" Richard asked.

"Oh gods no. Why would she?" Nicholas shuddered, the truth of Richard's question going straight over his head.

Holding Dickie's gaze, I shook my head. "Just a normal peace," I said.

A normal peace where Jace and everyone else would be safe.

Happy.

Jace...

SIXTEEN

A queen's duty is to her people.
May my life be my own in the next life.
- Aurelia

The week passed too swiftly. Despite having spent it laughing and playing with my brothers, with each passing day, my chest tightened to the point I could barely breathe. Slipping away as they played throwing knives – a target-based game I had played to utter exhaustion as it was Nicholas' favourite, I sat on a branch overlooking Brownston.

The brownies didn't seem so creepy from all the way up here...well, *as* creepy. Their music drifted up to me, soft and bouncy, so different to our screeching metal. A tear slipped down my cheek as I thought about home, about Jace... I wished he was here. Wished I could spend another moment with him before...

"Princess."

To Have and to Lose

Jerking on a twist, I nearly fell off the branch, but his arms were around me before I could even spread my wings. Hoisting me high, he walked us back from the edge before putting me down.

"What's wrong?" His eyes tracked the tear rolling down my cheek.

"Nothing."

"Princess..."

"What are you doing here?" I cut in, swiping at my face. "Why aren't you guarding Mother?"

"Her death is inevitable. Yours is not."

My heart lurching, I grabbed at his hand. "You can't stop Richard."

"Richard?"

Shit. He didn't know.

"I mean –"

His flash of confusion flickered into pain then betrayal then rage. Pulling away from me, he spread his wings and shot towards the trunk of the tree, towards the abandoned castle at which we were all staying.

"Jace!"

Scrambling after him, I flew as fast as I could. A broken scream echoed in front of me, burning every fibre of my being. I landed just in time to see him tackle Richard and plunge a knife into his hand, pinning him to the floor. Richard didn't fight back, just laid there in heartbreaking silence.

Kneeling over my brother's throat, Jace punched his best friend in the balls over and over and over again. I winced at each loud *thump*, at each crack of Jace's knuckles. At this rate, Richard would never be able to have heirs.

"You can't let him kill her!" Nicholas shouted from the other side of the room, tears rolling down his cheeks.

"How could you do this, Dick? How could you! She's our sister!"

Shaking his head, he backed away, not trying to stop Jace at all, giving him his silent support.

Jace lifted his fist and slammed it down again on Richard's crotch. He hit him so hard I felt as if I could feel the floor vibrating under my feet. And still Richard didn't fight back. Realising Jace would actually kill him, I charged forward.

"Leave him alone!" Grabbing Jace's shoulders, I started to pull him off, but he just kicked at Richard instead. "He's following my orders!"

The entire room froze.

The only sound was my beating pulse.

The only movement was Jace shaking beneath my fingers.

"What?" Slowly turning to face me, he looked into my eyes. "*What do you mean?*"

Desperation and pain reflected back at me.

My voice trembling, my heart aching, I filled him in on everything.

Dinner was understandably tense. Richard pushed around his food with his right hand, his left un-bandaged and still bleeding. My stomach churned up, I pushed my food around as well. Nicholas cried beside me, not even pretending to be okay. He hadn't known why we were really here. Hadn't known that this week was nothing but a goodbye.

Glancing across the table, I looked at Jace. He was still glaring at Richard, but at least he'd put down the spoon. I didn't know how much damage he could do with one, but

To Have and to Lose

I'd seen him kill with a blade of grass before...

Unable to bear the tension any longer, I stood up. The three quickly copied me – Richard with a painful wince.

Swallowing down the lump in my throat, I said, "I'd like to be alone."

Turning, I headed for my room, reminding myself that a queen's duty was to her people.

But gods, let me have my own life in the next.

Jace...

The knock on my door an hour later wasn't surprising. Richard had visited me every night before bed to talk and then sing me to sleep. Making memories.

Brushing at my face, I put on a smile and opened the door. I didn't want him to remember me sad.

My smile slipped.

Jace stood in front of me, his eyes as red as his bloody knuckles. He pushed his way inside, then kicked the door shut behind him. "Was I just going to be told the same lie as everyone else?"

"Jace..."

"Answer the question, princess." He moved closer, his words low and dangerous.

Despite the hammering of my heart, I met his gaze. "We didn't tell Nicholas."

His face twisted as I knew it would, his pain seemingly shared between us. "Don't compare me to your fucking brother. I'm –"

He stopped, holding my heart along with his breath. His silence.

I wanted so badly for him to finish that sentence, to voice what he was to me. And gods, I also didn't. Nothing could come of knowing. Nothing but pain. Stepping back, I hugged my waist, his mere proximity burning my skin, making me want things I couldn't want without breaking.

"I didn't want you to hate him. He needs you," I said softly, needing to put words between us. Anything to break the terrible silence.

"But he wouldn't if you just thought about this with a clear head. We can kill Seqora for you. We can –"

I placed my hand on his chest, stopping him from saying anything more. From convincing me that I could be queen. Because as much as I wanted to believe it in this moment, life wasn't a fairytale. *My decisions* had caused the death of tens of thousands of people. I had to save them from me as much as I had to save them from my psycho sister.

Fighting back tears, I ran my hand up to his cheek. He closed his eyes as he pushed against my palm.

"*Princess...*"

I stared at him, at the raw torment on his face, at the broken, hopeless pain and felt each shard pierce my heart. My eyes tracking him, I committed his every freckle, his every hair to memory. People said you didn't lose your memories in the afterlife, only upon rebirth. And if you could focus on someone strong enough, when you got reincarnated, you would be pulled to their soul. I wanted to believe that so fucking badly; I wanted to see Jace again. I wanted to get married without the weight of a royal wedding. I wanted kids that looked like him and laughter and peace.

"Will you smile for me?" I asked, knowing that this moment would be the one to stay with me forever. Every day – if there were still such things as days and nights in the afterlife – I would be cut apart by his pain and the guilt over doing nothing to ease his torment.

To Have and to Lose

He shuddered, a wretched, choked sob escaping his lips. Reaching forward, he crushed me in a hug, his arms the only things holding my heart together. Wet from tears, his mouth found mine. He smiled against me – a broken wet smile that tore apart the last of my resolve.

Drowned dreams streaming down my face, I gasped against him. I didn't care what our relationship was defined as. Whether we were just two friends saying goodbye or if we were something more, something that had never been voiced in fear of losing each other to war – a possibility we had witnessed time and time again. All that mattered was he was in my arms, and I was committing every particle of him to memory.

My tongue slid into his mouth.

There was a moment where time froze. Where he stilled beneath me, his only movement his heart beating against my chest.

And then he was kissing me back, his tongue stroking, his hands claiming, his wings spreading as he lifted us both into the air, as if he wanted to be the only thing touching me. As if he didn't want to share me with anything at all.

Or maybe that was my own projections.

Desperately, I wrapped my legs around his waist and tugged at the knot of his tunic, needing to feel his skin against mine, needing there to be nothing between us. With frantic tugs, he pulled at my clothes. His tongue inside me, he shoved off my top and cupped both breasts. I sucked in a gasp, the new sensations rocking me. Or maybe that was just him. The connection. The buzzing electricity between us.

His tunic now gone, I attacked his trousers. Our bodies dipped close to the floor before he flew us up. A bit too high, he bumped us into the ceiling.

"*Fuck.*"

Laughing through the pain, I managed to get him completely naked. And then I was grasping his cock and lifting myself up over it.

"Wait," he said, pulling away from my mouth for the first time since we'd started.

Whimpering, I found the strength to listen.

His fingers moved between us. "I have to check if you're ready. It can hurt and –"

Deciding it couldn't hurt more than my headache or the pain in my chest, I pushed down onto his cock. He hissed through his teeth and so did I because fuck, rug burn down there was not nice. But to hel if I was stopping. Gripping his shoulders, I spread my wings and moved myself up and down. Eventually, the burn subsided, and with his hands on my ass and his tongue back in my mouth, I quickened the pace.

His breaths started coming faster. When he leaned down to kiss my neck, I arched back, delighting in the friction of the new angle. I slammed down onto his cock, lifted off, then slammed down again...only to hear a loud crack and a scream as his cock hit my inner thigh.

His wings no longer flapping, we crashed into a crumbled heap on the floor.

"Jace!"

Half groaning, half laughing, he pushed me off him. "Fuck me, princess. How long were you waiting to pull that prank?"

Confused as all hel, I blinked at him. Then I realised he was cupping himself.

"Did I hit you in the balls?" I asked, burning with embarrassment.

"I wish."

"You wish..." I trailed off, suddenly feeling nauseous as

To Have and to Lose

I realised my thigh hurt quite a bit. From his cock. Knuckles cracked when they hit something that hard... "Oh my gods, did I break it?" When he didn't answer, I started to panic. "Jace, let me see it. Jace!"

Breathing out long and hard, he slowly removed his hands.

"Hel's tits!" It was snapped in half. I'd snapped Jace's dick. It was at a ninety degree angle in the wrong direction. He liked pain, but this was... This was... Oh my gods, I was going to be sick.

"Breathe, princess. Just relish in your victory."

"You're teasing me? Jace, I broke your dick!"

"It's fine," he wheezed. "I'll just get a healing wand and we can con–"

"We didn't bring one!" I shouted before lowering my voice in case my brothers heard. "Oh my gods, what are we going to do now?"

He raised both hands in the air and wiggled his fingers. "I've got ten more things you can break."

"Jace!"

He grinned. "You're right. My tongue is clearly the best option."

"But –"

"Shut it, princess. I'm not letting my own cock fucking cockblock me." Grabbing my hips, he pulled me to him. Too flabbergasted to resist, I ended up on his face. And then his tongue was inside me, his arms were wrapped around me, holding me *all* the way down, and the image of his broken cock was replaced by blinding stars.

I moaned against him, rocking my hips against his tongue. He licked between my labia, rubbing his lips against mine. Digging my fingers into his fine blond hair, I gripped him hard, my breaths leaving me on sharp, uncontrollable gasps. I rocked against him faster. He cherished me harder. But as his nose pressed against my clit and my body started to buzz, my thighs squeezing tight around him, I froze.

Oh my gods, what if I suffocate him?
I'd already snapped his dick.
And then I'd have to explain to Richard how I'd killed his best friend. Suffocated with a broken dick.

Pushing on Jace's head, I tried to shift my weight off him, but his arms tightened around me, holding me still. My heart hammering, I flapped my wings as a horrible thought filled my mind. What if he was trying to commit suicide to die with me?

His grip loosened immediately upon hearing my whimper. "Princess?" His voice soft, he lifted me up so he could wiggle out and look me in the eyes.

"Hey," he murmured as he reached up and cupped my cheek. "Am I moving too fast?"

"I thought you couldn't breathe."

"You thought I couldn't..." He laughed sharp and carefree, and tears glistened in my eyes over getting to hear him genuinely laugh one more time. "Princess, you can damn well bet I'm not going to let myself die before I'm inside you again."

"But your cock –"

His hands caressed my ass. "After I make you come all over my face, we're flying into Brownston to see a healer. Then I'm going to make you come all night."

I wanted to tell him I didn't think flying down there was a good idea, but as my mouth opened, he pulled me down *all* the way. His tongue stroked inside me, his hands spreading me open so he could plunge deeper. Moans left me rather than words, and I dug my fingers into his hair.

As he built me up higher and higher, I flapped my wings so fast a buzz filled the room. I shook against him.

To Have and to Lose

He held me tight. And when I screamed his name, he slipped a finger inside and curled it, hitting a spot that made me jerk on his face.

My shudders finally easing, I panted over him. His eyes held mine from between my thighs, and I ran my fingers softly through his hair. My chest expanded with so many emotions, so many regrets concerning a future we would never have. As tears filled my eyes, I looked away.

He reached up and cupped my cheek, his thumb feathering beneath my eye. Scooting me down his body, he sat up under me, wincing only slightly.

Remembering his broken penis, I started to climb to my feet, up off him, but he grabbed my hips and kept me there.

"You okay?"

I nodded, not trusting the words in my throat to stay down. There was no point voicing those three little words. All they would do was birth more pain.

"Let's go get you fixed," I said softly.

He grinned and blooped my nose. "You'll need something a lot stronger than a healing wand to do that, princess."

Pulling away from him, I rolled my eyes, a hint of a smile curling my lips. He was absolutely perfect...

Heading for my window, we opened it and spread our wings. Sneaking out of the abandoned castle, we flew down to the colourful mushroom-shaped houses of Brownston. We were greeted with shouts of joy and an orgy thrown in our honour – though really, brownies did not need a reason to have an orgy. They had them constantly. Sex was all they ever seemed to think about.

Ignoring the memories of the corpse-puppet vagina play, I approached the only person not currently fucking. "Do you know if anyone has a healing wand?"

She smiled at me, nodding enthusiastically. "I do! It's in the bathroom. Are you in pain?" She picked up a small rock on the table behind her.

A shiver raced down my spine from the way she looked at us, her eyes staring vacant.

"Not really," Jace said, a clear lie given he was looking a lot paler than he had a few minutes ago. He'd clearly caught on to whatever creepy silent question hadn't been asked.

"Where's the bathroom?" I just wanted to heal Jace and leave.

Putting down the rock, she led us through the house, past squirming, moaning bodies that all said hello to us. Once I had the healing wand in my hands, I dropped in front of Jace and said, "Iactus." Every pre-made wand was activated with the same word.

He hissed out a breath as his cock straightened in front of me. Then he pulled me up from the floor and kissed me. I reached over to lock the door of the bathroom, not wanting the brownies' creepy sex to come anywhere near ours.

Pivoting, Jace placed me on the bathroom sink and slipped between my thighs. My arms around his neck, I held him close. He hardened against my stomach, and I bucked my hips, needing him inside me again, needing these memories to hold on to.

Closing my eyes, I breathed him in. Held him in my heart.

Recalling all his laughter, the sixteen years of history between us, I reached down and wrapped my fingers around his cock.

"Fuck, princess," he hissed, pushing into my hand.

I squeezed him as I angled my hips and guided him in. His fingers dug into my sides. Pure pleasure poured across his face, making him so fucking beautiful.

Rocking my hips, I went slower this time, careful not to hurt him. His hands cupped my breasts. His lips found mine. Soft and tender, we made love until I spasmed around him on a cry.

Groaning, he grabbed my ass and gave it a quick squeeze before lifting me off him. My legs weak, I moved exactly where he wanted me – leaning over the sink, my legs crossed as he pushed into me from behind. The joyful brownie music thrummed around us. He moved inside me faster, stroked me deeper as my orgasm still raced through.

As I clenched around him for the third time, I balled my hands against the sink and screamed.

"Fuck, princess, don't do that."

Looking behind me, I watched as he pulled out and came all over my back.

My breath caught. Tears burned my eyes as I realised what he meant. His eyes closed, his head back, he held his cock in his hand as it continued to spurt. He didn't come inside me...

He didn't come inside me so it'd just be me who died – not a child we might've had.

When I woke up in bed in the morning, Jace was gone.

But before I could find the energy to leave my room, he entered it with a tray full of food. Neither one of my brothers could cook, so I knew he'd made breakfast himself.

He also made lunch.

And tea.

Sitting beside him come evening, one hand under the

table, holding his, I dug into the peppered bat wings, trying not to cry. I didn't want to tell him I'd only ever pretended to love them. But watching him eat them with a fake gusto across from my two brothers, they became my favourite food.

Nicholas smiled at me softly, his eyes red and swollen. He'd clearly cried all night, but today, he'd done his best to smile in my presence. He'd even joked and laughed between his nonstop stories about life at the castle while we'd been at war. He'd met someone – a woman named Dorothy, and she was super pretty. Even better, she was a baker of fine sweets.

I grinned back at him as I reached for my glass of wine. His sudden joke about brownies being yondus reincarnated made me spit it everywhere.

Laughing, I dotted up the mess with a serviette. Catching something flicker across Richard's face, I froze for just a second, my breath catching. My eyes landed on the wine seeping into the wood.

Glancing up to look at him fully, I reached for the bottle to refill my glass.

Pain twisted his brow. His eyes shining, he mouthed, "I love you."

As Jace's hand tightened around mine, I brought my new glass to my lips and drank it all.

Turning my head, I smiled at Jace and promised myself I would come back to him.

Whatever deal I had to make with Hel, I *would* make it back.

To him.

To us.

Leaning my head against his shoulder, I closed my eyes.

And held on tight to our memories.

EPILOGUE

Upon reincarnation, you get to fall for
your first love all over again.

Hello, stranger.
- Ember

Trailing the tattoo wand over my client's skin, I drew the final roots of the Yggdrasil tree curving around his left calf. The full body piece had taken me months to do – shading in the branches up his arms and neck, the twisted trunk across his torso, and finally, the roots across his legs.

Finished, I showed the Okahi actor to the mirror, where he marvelled at the highly detailed piece he'd drawn and I had transferred onto his glimmering blue exoskeleton. Clicking his mandibles, he voiced his appreciation as the bell over my door rang. His bulbous black eyes tracked the man entering, as did mine.

Although us, Vylians, and Okahi were finally at peace after centuries of war and there was free trade and open borders between our lands, tensions were still high between the races.

"I'll be with you in a second," I said, keeping my voice light and friendly even as I shifted warily onto the balls of my feet. It had been years since I'd been in combat, but I would fight for every one of my clients. This shop was my life, and I'd be damned if I let some racist fucker trash it.

"Take your time," the man murmured, meeting my gaze in the mirror.

My pulse kicked into my throat as I was snagged on the brilliant teal of his eyes. His short blond hair gleamed with sweat. Wrinkling my nose, I turned around to face him. "You smell," I said before I'd even thought the words.

I blinked in surprise.

So did he.

And then he smiled. "You smell *good*," he murmured, his eyes searching mine...no, not my eyes. *Me*. My very soul.

My breath caught.

My stomach fluttered.

Wetting my lips, I inhaled sharply at the sudden heat in his gaze. "Was there something I could do for you?" I asked, my words husky, my ears burning as I heard just how that sounded.

"Yeah. I want a tattoo on my thigh."

He unbuttoned his trousers, and I curled my toes inside my boots. Ever so slowly, he pulled the material down, and I couldn't look away even if I wanted to.

But the sight I was captivated by wasn't the lean, corded muscles of his thighs. Or the growing bulge above.

It was the large, colourful tattoo nestled on his left.

"What the fuck is that?" I laughed, unable to help myself, my eyes glued onto the large colourful image of an ass and a cock doing their business.

To Have and to Lose

Warmth in every word, he murmured, "A cherished memory."

AUTHOR'S NOTE

Hello everyone!

Thank you so much for reading *To Have and to Lose*. I hope you've fallen in love with these two just as much as I have, and I promise you Jace and Aurelia will get their happily ever after.

Richard's comes first though. Then Nicholas'.

But Aurelia does reappear in book two: *For Better or For Worse...* Major apologies beforehand. And that's why the epilogue wasn't in Jace's POV. There would've been massive spoilers...

Many cheers and hope you enjoy the rest of the series,

PS: A special shout-out to the Koala Hospital in Port Macquarie, Australia. It's an absolutely fantastic non-profit that focuses on the conservation of, surprise, koalas. If anyone else can spare any change, please do! https://shop.koalahospital.org.au/

5 REASONS TO SIGN UP TO MY NEWSLETTER OR JOIN MY FACEBOOK GROUP

1. Have the chance to name one of my characters!
2. Have the chance to join either my beta/ARC reader team.
3. Have the chance to pick which book I write next/which series I prioritise.
4. Download sneak preview chapters.
5. Get all the latest information about upcoming releases.

Sign me up now!

https://mirandagrant.ck.page/0e074e4e9c (direct)
https://mirandagrant.co.uk (sign-up form)
https://www.facebook.com/groups/900675603963724 Readers of the Myth (FB group)

3 REASONS TO LEAVE A REVIEW

1. They give me the strength and confidence to keep writing. The more reviews, the faster I write.
2. Chance to see your reviews inside one of my books.
3. I will love you forever.

Lightning Source UK Ltd.
Milton Keynes UK
UKHW041850060223
416533UK00001B/161